4 hackey books to Tyvan and Emily June 2007.

Interference

Lorna Schultz Nicholson

James Lorimer & Company Ltd., Publishers
Toronto

James Lorimer & Company Ltd. acknowledges the support of the Ontario Arts Council. We acknowledge the support of the Government of Canada through the Book Publishing Industry Development Program (BPIDP) for our publishing activities. We acknowledge the support of the Canada Council for the Arts for our publishing program. We acknowledge the support of the Government of Ontario through the Ontario Media Development Corporation's Ontario Book Initiative.

Cover illustration: Greg Ruhl

The Canada Council   Le Conseil des Arts
  for the Arts   du Canada

ONTARIO ARTS COUNCIL
CONSEIL DES ARTS DE L'ONTARIO

Canada Cataloguing in Publication Data

Schultz Nicholson, Lorna
    Interference / written by Lorna Schultz Nicholson.

(Sports stories ; 68)
ISBN 1-55028-823-7 (bound)   ISBN 1-55028-822-9 (pbk.)

I. Title. II. Series: Sports stories (Toronto, Ont.); 68.

PS8637.C49I58 2004   jC813'.6   C2004-900524-3

James Lorimer & Company Ltd.,   Distributed in the United States by:
Publishers   Orca Book Publishers
35 Britain Street   P.O. Box 468
Toronto, Ontario   Custer, WA USA
M5A 1R7   98240-0468
www.lorimer.ca

Printed and bound in Canada.

Contents

Author's Note

I would like to thank my editor, Hadley Dyer, for her insight and enthusiasm, and my writer's group — Jacquie, Joan, Andrea, Kath and Patty — who have always provided encouragement and laughter. I am also grateful to Allison Husband from the Diabetes Clinic D.A.T. Centre at the Alberta Children's Hospital for reading my manuscript to ensure the medical information is correct. I owe a big thank you to Sean Borbridge and his mother, Maria, for welcoming me into their home and allowing me to barrage them with questions about diabetes, and to Bob Clarke, who was/is a hockey player with diabetes, for taking the time out of his busy schedule to read my manuscript. And last, but not least, I would like to thank my husband, Bob, for making sure the hockey end was up to snuff, and my children, Mandi, Marijean and Grant, for making sure my story was good enough for their friends to read.

— *Lorna Schultz Nicholson*

To my mother and father,
Mary and Art Schultz,
with love

1

Late for Practice

Josh Watson sat on the end of his bed and plugged his ears. He hated the fighting. No matter how hard he tried to muffle the voices, however, Josh could still hear his father from the kitchen.

"You are not missing a hockey game to go to a party, Matt; you're still grounded. And that's final!"

"You said I was only grounded from driving your car! Why can't I go to the party?" Matt slammed something. Josh couldn't tell if he had banged a cupboard door or hit a notebook against the wall.

"I'm not impressed with those kids, Matt. I bet none of your hockey friends are going. Don't you even care about the team?"

"Of course I care! But what is the big deal if I miss one game? Coach won't bench me. I'm too good."

"Don't take your talent for granted, young man." Mr. Watson sounded close to breaking. "I saw Jason Penner squealing his father's tires in the parking lot. You are not hanging out with that group, especially after your latest speeding ticket. Focus on your hockey."

"Here we go again. Didn't you ever drive fast when you were young!?" Matt yelled.

Josh waited until he heard the stomping footsteps pass his room and Matt's bedroom door slam before he picked up his new hockey stick from the corner. The fight was over for now — until Matt asked to go to another party or drove like a maniac again.

Josh ran his hand up and down the Synergy stick. He had saved all his birthday and dog-sitting money to buy this stick and couldn't wait to use it. He'd been practising his shots outside, hitting hundreds of pucks against the garage door. He just hoped this new stick would help him rip the puck in the top corner today at practice.

Josh checked the time on his clock radio. The fight between his brother and dad had lasted longer than usual. Now he was going to be late for hockey practice. His stomach twisted into knots.

When Josh first made the Stingers, he was ecstatic. Not only was it the best Pee Wee Team in his minor hockey association, it was the first year he had ever made the top team in his division. He'd worked all summer to get fit, inline skating up and down the Calgary bike paths. Plus, he'd gone to *two* summer hockey camps! In September, he'd stepped on the ice for evaluations feeling more confident than ever. He skated hard and was the last player chosen to make the team.

Josh soon found out, however, that being the bottom player wasn't always fun. Last practice they had skated the circles, and even though Josh had started in the middle, he had been lapped. It's as if he had peaked in September, before the season even started. Lately, he seemed so tired all the time! He used to be able to keep up with most of the other players on the team, but now he was the slowest. Were they getting better, or was he just getting worse?

He sighed and closed his bedroom door, hoping his dad had cooled down by now. Josh also knew his father couldn't handle him being the worst player on the team. He'd seen his dad in the stands with his arms crossed, shaking his head.

At first Josh's dad had shown up to all his practices — even gone on the ice to help Coach Jim. Recently, though, Dad had stopped coming. Josh knew part of the reason was the problem his parents were having with Matt. Matt had always been a star, but now he seemed to be losing interest in hockey, which upset Dad.

When Josh entered the kitchen, he could see only the top of his dad's head — the same strawberry-red hair Josh had inherited. Mr. Watson sat at the table, elbows on the table, head in his hands.

"Dad," he said quietly.

His dad looked up. "What is it, son?"

"I have practice today. It starts at 2:00."

Josh's dad ran his hand through his hair and sighed. "I'm sorry. I forgot. Where's your equipment?"

"In the garage."

"Put it in the car; I'll take you over now."

"Maybe Mom can drive me," Josh suggested, not wanting to put any more pressure on his dad. Matt did enough of that. Josh couldn't figure Matt out. He was the best hockey player on his team — in the league even — but it was like he wanted to party instead of play hockey. Josh would do anything to have his brother's talent ... to make his father *want* to take him to practice.

"Your mom's picking up Amy from dance class. Get your equipment and I'll take you."

Josh put his bag in the back of the SUV, and got in the front seat to wait for his father. He could see his breath swirling from the cold air. He rubbed his hands together, wishing his dad would hurry up. The weather had changed from fall to winter almost as soon as the calendar had flipped from November to December. A few flurries had fallen overnight.

Josh scraped the ice on the side window with his fingernail. Where was his dad? He kept looking at his watch. He was going to be so late getting on the ice! Eight minutes passed before his dad slammed the front door shut.

"Sorry, Josh," he said, starting the engine.

"It's okay." Josh looked straight ahead out the window.

"Your brother just infuriates me. He's wasting his talent. He's sixteen and he could be on his way to a college scholarship or Juniors, even the pros if he'd put his mind to it." His father drove faster than normal.

"I'm not making a rink for him this year. He just doesn't deserve it."

Josh clutched the door handle, remaining silent. His dad went on and on about Matt. For as long as Josh could remember, his father had made an outdoor rink. Matt and Josh used it all winter, but last year, Josh spent the most time on it. Matt was everything Josh wasn't — big, strong, fast and blond. Josh was puny, skinny with red hair and freckles.

As they approached the arena, his dad headed to the front drop-off instead of the parking lot.

"Are you coming in?" asked Josh.

"Not today. I've got to go home and talk some sense into Matt. Do you think you can get a ride home?"

Josh shrugged. "Sure. Kaleigh's mom or dad can take me. One of them is always here."

Josh's dad unlocked the doors from inside the vehicle. "Have a good practice."

"Thanks, Dad."

Josh had barely pulled his equipment from the trunk before his dad drove off. He sighed, knowing his father *never* missed Matt's practices. Once his dad's vehicle was out of sight, Josh ran as fast as he could into the arena.

2

Lousy Shot

H ey, Watson," said Eric, the captain of the Springland Stingers, when Josh pushed open the door to the dressing room, "you're late."

"Sorry," Josh began. "My dad—"

"We don't want to hear your lame excuses." Eric was already tying his skates. Eric had been picked as captain at the beginning of the season and was taking his job seriously.

Josh looked around the crowded room. When you arrived late there was no space left to get dressed.

"Here's space, Josh. Hurry." Kaleigh, the only girl on the team and the best girl hockey player in Calgary, moved down and pointed to a spot beside her on the bench.

Josh threw his hockey bag on the floor and pulled out his long johns. Kaleigh always arrived fully dressed and didn't enter the room until the guys at least had long johns, shin-pads and socks on.

Josh took a deep breath. He really didn't want Kaleigh to see his body. He *had* to leave his boxers on. When he glanced at her out of the corner of his eyes, he noticed she was bending over, tying her skates, and her honey-colored hair had fallen forward to hide her face.

Josh was still tying up his skates when everyone else was

rounding the first lap of warm-up. As he stepped on the ice, he heard Coach Jim's voice.

"Josh, I want one quick lap around the ice. Get moving."

Josh knew the entire team was watching him so he pushed his legs as hard as he could, but his legs felt like rubber. He skated back into the team circle breathing hard, his chest moving up and down. At summer hockey camp, he had never been winded like this.

"Ever thought of a training program?" muttered Eric under his breath.

Josh tried to ignore Eric as he listened to Coach Jim explain a controlled breakout drill. He crossed his fingers that he wouldn't be on Eric's line today. Eric only passed the puck at the beginning of the drill — never at the end of the drill. He always took the shot on net. Josh wanted to try his new stick. He wanted to be the one to shoot it in over the goalie's shoulder. He'd show Eric how much he had practised!

"Yes!" Josh cheered, punching the air with his fist when he heard he was with Kaleigh and Tony. Tony was the assistant captain and one of the few players who didn't seem to mind being on a line with him. Sometimes he even passed the puck to Josh.

The first time down the ice, Josh, as left winger, didn't get the puck as they broke out of their own end and through the neutral zone. Tony, at centre ice, passed to Kaleigh on right wing. She drove to the net, making a drop pass to Tony who was in the slot. Tony one-timed it in the corner of the net. Although Sam, the Stingers' goalie, reached out with his catching glove to stop the puck he still missed it.

"Nice shot, Tony," said Josh when they were lined up again, waiting their turn.

"Thanks," Tony replied.

After repeating the drill five times, Josh still hadn't taken a shot on net.

He turned to Kaleigh and said, "Instead of making a drop pass to Tony, why don't you try hitting me at the hash marks. Or drop pass it to Tony and I'll drive to the net to deflect it in. Let me make the shot."

She nodded and explained the play to Tony.

When it was their line's turn, Tony passed to Kaleigh in the neutral zone. Josh skated down his wing. Once over the blue line, he drove to the net. Instead of drop passing the puck to Tony, Kaleigh looked up, saw Josh and made a perfect pass to him. Josh kept his feet moving and let his shot rip. He thought he heard a crack, but instead he saw the puck dribble toward the net and Sam bat it out of the way. Josh smacked his stick on the ice. What a lousy shot! Tony got the rebound and took another shot.

Coach Jim blew the whistle, signalling the players to skate as hard as they could to centre ice. The last one there had to do laps. Unfortunately, Josh was behind the net, farthest away from centre ice. Even though he made a tight turn and dug in his edges, he still ended up last to the circle.

"Quick lap, Josh. You know the rules."

After skating his lap, Josh, knowing his face under his cage was as red as the Canadian flag, ended up beside Eric. He got down on one knee to listen to Coach Jim.

"Why are you always the last one?" hissed Eric, leaning into Josh.

Josh tried to ignore him. Instead he concentrated on Coach Jim who was praising everyone's effort and demonstrating Drill Number Two on the white board.

"And you need some muscle on the puck," continued Eric.

Josh was so thirsty. And tired! Tired of Eric always picking on him and tired of being the worst one on the team. Why wasn't he getting better?

Josh was first out of his equipment and first out of the dressing room. He couldn't stand knowing that he was the lousiest player on the team. He just wanted to go home before his team mates swarmed out to the lobby. Josh saw Kaleigh's dad standing by the bulletin board.

"Hi, Mr. Radcliffe," he said, pulling his bag behind him.

"Hey, Josh. That was a tough practice. You made some good passes out there."

"Thanks. I just wish I could put the puck in the net."

"Don't worry. It'll come." Mr. Radcliffe patted Josh on the back. "We've got our outdoor rink almost ready. You're welcome to use it any time. I ran into your dad the other day, and he said he wasn't going to make one this year."

Josh shrugged, feeling tongue-tied talking to an adult. He glanced around the lobby, stalling for time. He hated asking for a ride home.

"Mr. Radcliffe," he started, only to be interrupted by Kaleigh who had somehow appeared out of nowhere.

"May I have some money for a drink, Dad?" Kaleigh asked, her hand stretched out, palm up.

"How hard did you work?"

Kaleigh playfully punched her dad's shoulder. "Come on, Dad. Please? I only need a couple of bucks." She smiled sweetly and her dad shook his head, reaching into his pants pocket for some change.

Josh followed Kaleigh to the vending machine.

"Can I get a ride with you?" he whispered.

"Sure." Kaleigh bobbed her head and inserted two coins in the slot. "My dad won't mind."

"Mind what?" Eric stood behind Kaleigh in the machine

line-up. He had one of those early January birthdays and was the tallest — and oldest — on the team.

"Driving Josh home." Kaleigh swung her hair when she turned and smiled.

"Where's *your* dad?" Eric looked directly at Josh. "Does your brother have a game?"

"Not 'til later," said Josh.

"It's hard to believe you two come from the same family." Eric dropped his money in the machine and pressed the button for Coke.

"Why do you say that?" asked Kaleigh.

"Duh. His brother is so good and he's so lou-sy." Eric widened his eyes when he spoke.

"Stop being a jerk, Eric," said Kaleigh.

Eric flipped the tab on his pop. "My sister says he's one of the funniest guys at the high school too. He's in her drama class. Supposedly he's the best actor in the class — in the whole high school for that matter."

"My brother?" Josh couldn't believe that.

"Yeah, he's obviously nothing like you."

"Eric!" Kaleigh frowned. "That's mean."

"Look, I'm not the captain of this team to be Mr. Nice Guy. The Stingers have a chance to win the city championships this year. My role is to help us win. Ever heard the saying, 'you're only as good as your weakest player?'" He glanced accusingly at Josh.

"Leave him alone, Eric."

"What, he can't stand up for himself?"

"Stop it, Eric," said Kaleigh. "Come on, Josh. Let's go."

When they were outside Kaleigh said, "Eric's full of it. Don't listen to him."

"I try not to. The truth is, he's right." Josh sighed. "I am getting worse."

3

Big Brother, Little Sister

All the way home in the Radcliffe's car, Josh looked longingly at Kaleigh's drink. He'd just downed an entire bottle of water, but was still feeling thirsty. He'd never had to drink so much, or stop so much as he did today in practice. He used to be able to play continuously; now he couldn't make it through one drill. Then again, these practices were harder. Josh swallowed; his mouth was dry.

"Kaleigh, I was telling Josh that our rink is almost ready to skate on," said Mr. Radcliffe.

"Just a few more days, right dad?" said Kaleigh. She turned to Josh. "Come on over any time. I'll be out there just about every day that we don't have practice."

Josh nodded as he drew little squiggly lines on his jeans. The lump in his throat felt huge. He'd like to practise with Kaleigh, if only he was playing better.

"I could ... help you." Kaleigh said quietly. "I took power skating last year and I remember what the instructor taught me. I even made notes."

Josh slowly nodded his head. "Okay," he said, "I need all the help I can get."

* * *

Josh and Amy set the dinner table. Josh could barely stand listening to his ten-year-old sister go on about her dance competition and the bi-i-g trophy she had won. He thought it was the ugliest trophy he'd ever seen — brassy thing that looked like it belonged in a second-hand store.

"It doesn't look new," he said, putting down five forks. The Watsons rarely ate dinner together because of their crazy schedules.

"Well, it is new!" she said pertly.

"Yeah, right."

"You're just mad 'cause you've never gotten a trophy as big as mine." Amy thumped the last plate down and stomped into the kitchen, her red pony-tail swinging with her stride. At least she didn't have her hair in that stupid bun she always wore for dance.

Josh could hear her telling on him. "Tattle tale!" he muttered under his breath. He thought he heard the word "jealous" come from his mother. Brother! He wasn't jealous of Amy's dance. Last year, Josh's team had been in three tournaments and won some top awards. He couldn't care less about her trophy!

Josh's favourite dinner was lasagna and tonight it looked great — bubbling with cheese. He was so hungry that he took two huge helpings, even though he knew that his mom had baked a cake for dessert. As famished as he was, he was sure he could eat both.

"Josh, you're hungry tonight," his mom observed.

"No junk food at the rink?" asked his dad.

"I didn't have any money," said Josh, wanting his parents to feel guilty for not picking him up.

"It's good to see you're hungry. Does that mean you worked hard at practice?" His dad ripped the crust off a piece of garlic toast.

"I tried ... It was a good practice," said Josh, filling up his water glass for the fourth time. "We did this neat breakout drill."

Mr. Watson acknowledged his comment with a nod, then turned to Matt. "You need to be strong in the offensive end, Matt; that's what those scouts will be looking for — a goal scorer. Put a few in the net and they'll want you next year. They'll remember you if you're good and you get points."

Matt looked down at his plate and shovelled a huge forkful of lasagne in his mouth. Silence filled the air, except for the sound of silverware scraping the plates. Josh finished his food while looking at Matt, wondering why he wasn't more enthusiastic about this. Matt was on one of the Triple-A Midget teams — comprised of the best 15- and 16-year-old players in the North side of Calgary! They were entered in a huge tournament where the top teams from Canada came to play. Scouts from the Major Junior League and the American NCAA Colleges were flying in to see who was going to be the next star. Matt stood a chance at making a Major Junior team or maybe getting a college scholarship.

"Don't you agree with me, Matt?" asked his dad.

"I guess," said Matt, finally making eye contact with his dad for a second. Then he turned to Amy with his Jim Carrey impersonation, "Hey, Cindy-Lou Hoo, pass the roast beast. I mean salad, would yah?"

Amy giggled and handed the big wooden bowl to Matt. "Did you see my trophy, Matt?"

"Hard to miss," said Matt, winking at her. "That's awesome, kiddo." This time he had spoke in a cowboy drawl. "What did you git it for?"

"My jazz solo." Amy thrust her chin upwards and flicked her head.

Josh thought he would throw up! "Can I eat my dessert in my room?" he asked. "I've got tons of homework to do."

Josh's mom nodded, so he took his plate to the kitchen, cut himself a big piece of chocolate cake, then scooted down the hall, taking the stairs two at a time to get to his room. He breathed a sigh of relief when he closed his door. Amy was so annoying and Matt thought he was so cool with those dumb impersonations.

Josh's room was decorated with posters of hockey players. His favourites were the Calgary Flames, Colorado and, of course, the Canadian Olympic Team. He'd watched every Olympic hockey game in 2002 and been so excited when they'd won the gold medal.

He sat at his desk and licked every last cake crumb from the plate. Somehow, sweets made him feel like he used to — more energetic. He pushed the plate aside and pulled out his homework.

He was entrenched in writing a report on his favourite book — *The Lord of the Rings* — when he heard a knock on his door. "Yeah," he said, without getting up from his desk.

Matt loped in and sat on Josh's bed.

"What do you want?" asked Josh, turning in his chair to stare at Matt.

"Have you ever read this?" Matt held up *Twelfth Night*, by Shakespeare.

Josh shook his head, but reached for the book. "Do you have to read it for English or something? 'Cause I can't write a report for you this time. Not Shakespeare."

Last year, Josh had written a report for Matt on *The Hobbit*, even though he had only been in Grade 7 and Matt was in Grade 10. It had been Josh's favourite book at the time, the prequel to *The Lord of the Rings*. Matt had actually gotten a decent mark on the report. Josh knew he'd changed a few words here and there, but still, it was his work.

"I don't need a report." Matt said indignantly. "I just wondered if you'd read it."

Josh shook his head, trying to figure Matt out. "Sorry. I like fantasy books."

Matt nodded, smacking his hand against the book. "You probably wouldn't understand it anyway. It's hard to read. The characters talk weird," Matt put his hand to his chest, "saying 'thee' and 'thou' all the time." He dropped his hand and looked at Josh. "Like I said, *you* probably wouldn't get it."

"Yeah, right. Since when have you liked reading?" asked Josh, shaking his head at Matt. Sometimes he was such a jerk.

"This is a play," said Matt sarcastically, puffing up his chest. "I'm auditioning for a part in the school play," Matt flicked his hair out of his eyes.

Josh rolled his eyes. "The *school play?*"

Matt glared at Josh as he shook his head. "Yeah. It's a rush being on stage. Sort of like scoring a big goal in hockey only better, way better."

"You're crazy. Nothing beats scoring a goal."

"Just think," Matt held his hand up in a pose. "My name in lights."

"Shakespeare is not impersonations, Matt." Everyone knew Matt as a hockey player, and not a smart one either. Josh got the good grades, not Matt. Granted, Matt could improve his marks if he tried a little harder.

"Have some faith," snapped Matt. "To me this is a challenge. Just you wait, I'll get the part of the Fool — the lead role. And he's big-time funny."

"How are you going to play hockey *and* be in the school play?"

"I'll figure it out." Matt stood.

"Does Dad know?" Josh asked, staring at Matt, who looked away.

"He'll say you can't, you know," Josh continued.

With his lips tight, eyebrows furrowed and eyes in a squint, Matt turned to look at Josh. "I don't care what he says. He doesn't rule my life!"

"Josh!" Mrs. Watson yelled.

"Yeah, Mom!" Josh pushed past Matt so he could see what she wanted.

"Kaleigh's on the phone." His mother seemed to sing-song the words as she shouted from the bottom of the stairs.

"You'd better get out there and answer the phone," said Matt sarcastically. "It's your gir-r-l-friend."

"She's not my girlfriend!" Josh shoved Matt out of his bedroom, suddenly feeling flushed and sweaty.

4

An Outdoor Skate

The next afternoon, Josh's mother dropped him off at Kaleigh's with his skates, stick, helmet and gloves. He didn't need full equipment.

Josh and Kaleigh put on their skates outside on a bench made of old hockey sticks. They both lived outside the city limits on one-acre lots. The houses were spread out, making lots of room for ice rinks.

The sky was as blue as a mountain lake and little white clouds dotted the horizon line. Josh kept blowing on his hands to keep them warm while he tied up his laces. Although it was cold, he knew the weather was perfect for playing hockey outdoors.

Josh stepped onto the ice, loving the crunching sound of his skates digging into the outdoor ice. And when his stick made contact with the puck, the smacking noise echoed through the poplar trees. The brisk air felt so refreshing on his face, especially after sitting in a stuffy classroom all day. He liked the tingling on his cheeks. The sun sat like a big ball in the sky and, although it was with them now, Josh knew in an hour it would be gone and the rink would be covered in shadows. Mr. Radcliffe had set up lights for night skating.

Josh glided with contentment on his skates, thinking about how much he loved hockey — everything about the sport.

Kaleigh and Josh played around for half an hour, shooting pucks and stick-handling up and down the ice. The rink was a good size, and Mr. Radcliffe had obviously worked night and day to make the ice as smooth as glass. The only bumps were along the sides. Kaleigh and Josh took turns trying to chop them up. Josh thought of his own father out flooding the rink late at night in the previous years. This year he had put the boards up but hadn't been out yet with the hose.

"Want me to show you some of the things I learned in advanced power skating?" Kaleigh asked Josh during a short break. Josh had brought a huge water bottle with him, and had already drank most of it.

"Sure," said Josh, wiping water from his mouth. "I only took beginner classes."

For the next hour, Kaleigh showed Josh what she knew. Digging the toes in while doing short strides at the beginning was important to getting a quick start. Also, using your edges was key. Kaleigh made Josh get low, like a sprinter at the start of a race. His legs had to move quickly; his body had to explode forward, then lift slowly as he started to lengthen his strides. If Josh came up too soon, Kaleigh told him to try again because the power would go upward instead of forward. Josh kept trying until his legs were burning and he desperately needed a break.

"Did that help?" asked Kaleigh.

"Yeah, thanks," said Josh. "I can't wait to try this tomorrow in our game."

Kaleigh looked at her watch. "Want to shoot some pucks? It's just five."

Josh's mom was coming at 6:00 on her way home from picking up Amy. He nodded his head. "Let's set up the cans so we have some targets."

"Better yet," Kaleigh smiled. "My dad just got me a Shooter Tooter."

"Cool!" said Josh.

After they had draped the blue plastic cover with the painted goalie on it over the net, and fastened it securely, they lined up all the pucks in a row. Five holes were cut as targets: one in each top corner, one in the lower middle (called the five hole) and two in the bottom corners.

Kaleigh went first, sinking her wrist shot in the five hole. Josh managed to sink the puck in the bottom right corner with his wrist shot, but not hard enough. They took turns. When it came to the top corner, Josh just couldn't raise the puck enough to get it in.

"Josh, what's the matter? You used to have such a good shot." Kaleigh skated over to him. "Maybe you're holding your stick different?"

Josh shrugged and got into position to take a slap shot. He wound up, bringing his stick back then swinging through the puck, shifting his weight with a follow through. Good shots were all in the timing. Josh's timing was off again. The puck lifted slightly off the ground, wobbled a bit, then hit the ice, hardly making it to the net.

"Maybe you should talk to Coach Jim. He may be able to help." Kaleigh started to pick up the pucks, throwing them in the bucket.

"Kaleigh, can I use your washroom?" Josh crossed his legs. Last night he'd had to go to the bathroom in the middle of the night.

"I want to go in too," she said. "It's getting dark and I'm cold. Let's pick up these pucks and call it a night."

Josh helped gather the pucks when all he wanted to do was run in the house. Finally, he sat down on the bench and took off his skates as fast as he could. He was finished both skates and

Kaleigh didn't even have one off yet.

"Can I just go in?" he asked.

Kaleigh pointed to the back door. "It's open. You shouldn't drink so much water."

Josh ignored her comment and ran to the back door, leaving his skates, gloves and helmet outside in the snow. Kaleigh was right, he should stop drinking so much water. Today at school, he'd had to go the bathroom after every class.

When Josh came out of the bathroom, Kaleigh called to him from the kitchen. He could hear the spoon clinking the mug. "I'm in here, Josh. I'm making hot chocolate."

Upon entering the kitchen, Josh saw the big container of instant hot chocolate, a bag of coloured marshmallows and a can of whipped cream. Kaleigh tipped the bottle of whipped cream, pressing the nozzle to make a hissing sound.

"Wow, gourmet chocolate." Josh grinned.

Kaleigh looked up and smiled back. Her cheeks were rosy from the cold and her hair hung loose. Josh couldn't help but think she was the prettiest girl in the school.

Josh burned his lips on the hot chocolate and sputtered, feeling like a fool.

Kaleigh laughed. "It's hot!" She opened the fridge door and pulled out two cans of pop. "Here," she said. "Want something to help wash it down?" She glanced around before putting her fingers to her mouth. "Just don't tell my mom, she'll kill me for drinking pop. She says it's just for weekends." Kaleigh rolled her eyes and gently pulled the tab to avoid fizz. "She's downstairs on the computer," she whispered.

Josh followed Kaleigh's lead and opened his pop the same way. He drank half of the can in one gulp.

Josh noticed Kaleigh staring at him. "Wow! Drink much? You're gonna get sick."

"Nah," said Josh. "I was just really thirsty. It tasted good after being outside."

"You're always thirsty."

"Did you get your reading project done?" he asked.

"Almost," said Kaleigh. "I still have to do one question — on homonyms and antonyms. You done that one yet?"

Josh was about to answer her when the phone rang. "My mom will get it," said Kaleigh.

Mrs. Radcliffe called upstairs. "Kaleigh? Telephone!"

Kaleigh went to the kitchen desk and picked up the portable. "Hello."

"Hi, Eric." She paused, looking at Josh.

Josh drank the rest of his pop and wiped his mouth when he was finished. His stomach felt funny. He wasn't sure if it was from the pop or the mention of Eric's name.

"Sure," said Kaleigh. "That sounds great. I'd love to go. I'll have to ask my mom first, though."

Josh looked around the kitchen, trying not to stare at Kaleigh or hear what she was saying to Eric. His head was spinning. Where were they going? Not somewhere fun, he hoped! Josh glanced at his watch. His mom would be here soon. He started to gather his things, suddenly remembering he'd left his skates outside.

He thumbed outside to Kaleigh. She waved to him, motioning him to stay. He took a deep breath, waiting for her to say good bye to Eric. Seconds later, she hung up the phone. "What's your hurry?" she asked.

"It's 6:00." Josh replied briskly. "My mom will be here soon."

"Okay."

"What did he want?"

She shrugged. "He invited me to a Flames game on the

weekend." Her eyes lit up. "I haven't been to one of their games yet this season."

"I need to get my gear from outside," said Josh walking to the door, his shoulders feeling heavy. He had a hard time looking Kaleigh in the eyes. "Thanks for the help. I'll see you tomorrow at school."

"And at our game!" said Kaleigh, giving him the thumbs up.

5

The Penalty Kill

The Stingers had been assigned Dressing Room 2 for their first away-game. Mrs. Watson dropped Josh off early so she could take Amy to dance before she came back to watch the last period. Mr. Watson was taking Matt to an important practice. He promised Josh that he'd come to his next game.

While waiting for the other players to arrive, Josh rolled up a hunk of black tape and batted it around with his stick. He took shots against the wall and stick-handled around the garbage pail that stood in the centre of the room. "He dekes around the first forward," Josh narrated, circling the pail. "He's heading down the ice, around the first defense, the second defense ... *Wham!* He shoots it top corner, right over the goalie's head." Josh shot the ball of tape at the door.

"Hey!" Eric ducked, narrowly avoiding the tape.

"Sorry," said Josh, grinning sheepishly.

Eric leaned his stick against the wall and wheeled his equipment over to the bench. "I can't wait to play this team. My friend from summer hockey school plays for the Crowsnest Cougars."

"Is he good?" asked Josh.

"Top scorer." Eric unzipped his bag. "But we can beat these guys." He glanced at Josh. "That is, if we all play hard."

"I'm ready," said Josh, sitting down to open his bag. He felt better today, especially after he drank a juice box. Maybe he'd just had a flu bug or cold? His throat was fine though. Whatever! Josh didn't care; he just wanted to have a good game today. Suddenly Sam barreled through the door with his massive goalie bag.

"Hiya, Sam!" Josh smacked Sam on the back as he made his way to the adjoining bathroom. He knew he'd better go before he got dressed. "We got to beat these guys today."

"Go, Stingers!" bellowed Sam.

"Yeah, Stingers!" yelled Eric as a few more guys entered the dressing room.

"Go, Stingers!" called Josh from inside the washroom.

Now Coach Jim's voice filled the room. "Okay, everybody, here's our strategy…"

* * *

The Stingers scored the first goal! And what a smooth move it had been by Eric. He passed to Brett, who was positioned at the side of the net. Brett deflected the puck, beating the goalie who really had no chance. The Stingers smacked the boards with their hands and cheered. Eric hugged Brett on the ice. "See guys, an assist is as good as a goal." Coach Jim applauded. "Instead of shooting straight at the goalie, Eric gave a pass and Brett timed it perfectly. Hockey is about moving the puck."

Josh stepped on the ice and skated to his wing, ready for the face-off. Kaleigh was playing centre and she peered over at him as if to say, *get ready*. Josh knew her strategy. She would get it back to the defense, Josh would skate to the boards and the defense would hit Josh on the wing. Josh would carry it up the wing and drop pass it to Kaleigh, who would either pass back or take a shot. The other winger was to drive to the net for the rebound.

Kaleigh managed to nail the face-off. Josh took off down his wing, saw the puck coming and, just when he had it on his stick, he felt the hit. Smacked into the boards, he fell hard. When he got up, he saw the Cougars had possession and were in the Stingers' end. Josh dug his toes in and skated as hard as he could to backcheck but he wasn't quick enough. Fortunately, Sam made a great save with his glove hand.

Josh skated up to the goalie. "Awesome save, Sam."

"Thanks." Sam skated his ritual skate around the back of the net and Josh made his way to the bench.

Coach Jim patted Josh on the back. "Keep your head up, Josh. You would have had him beat."

Josh nodded and grabbed his water bottle.

The Cougars scored the next goal on a breakaway. Sam didn't have a hope against Eric's friend, who ripped a wrist shot in the top corner. Now the game was tied, 1–1. Josh was relieved that he wasn't on the ice for the goal against. He didn't want to take any heat for messing up.

Mid-way through the second period, the Stingers got a tripping penalty. Josh's line was due out next.

"Josh, you sit." Coach Jim pointed to Kaleigh and Tony, motioning them to get on the ice.

Josh nodded. One day he'd like to be chosen to kill the penalty. Josh watched as his line-mates played the short-handed shift without him. Kaleigh was all over the ice, hustling — and it payed off! She intercepted a pass and ... had a break away. Josh cheered. "Go, Kaleigh!"

In an amazing move, she pulled the puck to the side, faking out the goalie, then she back-handed it in the corner of the net. The Stingers went wild!

"You did it! What a play!" Josh bonked the front of Kaleigh's helmet with his stick when she came to the bench. He wished he had been on the ice for the goal.

The score remained 2–1 for the rest of the second period. Josh played okay, but he missed a shot on net. It had been the perfect set-up. He was wide open, the pass had been right on his stick, but when he made the shot, he shot right at the goalie who saved it with no problem. If only he could have scored. Josh had scored only one goal all season.

Ten minutes into the third period, Josh knew he had to go the bathroom. He tried to breathe deep to stop the horrible feeling. This had never happened to him before. He must have drunk too much water. He shook his leg, tapped his foot but nothing helped. Oh, man. Why now? He knew he couldn't hold it any longer. He tapped Coach Jim on the arm. "I have to go to the can," he whispered

Coach Jim glanced incredulously at him. "*Now?*"

"Yeah."

The whistle blew. Another penalty. Interference.

"*Darn,*" said Coach Jim. "Josh, I wanted you to kill this penalty."

Josh squeezed his legs together. He knew he couldn't hold it. "I have to *go,*" he said in exasperation.

"All right, then." Coach Jim looked down the bench. "Kaleigh, Tony — you're on." Coach Jim opened the gate.

In the dressing room, Josh struggled with his hockey equipment. Thankfully, he had pants that didn't have suspenders. The pressure in his groin made his eyes water but he finally let out a huge sigh of relief.

Before Josh could get dressed again, he heard cheering coming from the bench. The Stingers must have scored again! When Josh pushed open the door, his team looked jubilant. Tony threw himself at Josh, practically knocking him over.

"*What a team!*"

"Where were you, Watson?" Eric scowled. "Having a nap?"

The rest of the team burst into laughter. Josh crumbled. He'd missed the extra point because he was busy in the washroom, *and* he blew his one chance to help kill the penalty.

There were only five minutes left in the game. He'd missed most of the third period. Josh shook his head. How can you play hockey when you're in the washroom? This hadn't happened to him since he was in Tyke.

6

Fight with Amy

The elated mood in the dressing room did little to perk Josh's spirits. He'd missed his first chance to penalty kill. He bent over to untie his skates, desperately fighting back the tears. If he cried there would be no end to the ridicule.

"So where *did* you go, Watson?" Eric persisted. "I don't see a pillow or a blankie."

Everyone laughed. Josh gulped. He knew he had to look up sometime. He took a deep breath and shrugged. "I knew you could beat the Cougars by yourself, Eric."

"That's where you're wrong." Eric stood. "I may be captain but we play as a team!" He thrust his arm in the air in victory.

Everyone cheered.

Eric stared at Josh. "Next time, don't leave…"

"My dad's buying slushies!" Kaleigh interrupted. She already had her skates off. Josh knew she was helping him save face and he wanted to thank her, but not now. He'd wait until they were in the lobby. She smiled and walked to the door, still in her gear.

"See you in the lobby, guys," she said, waving.

Josh undressed in record time and shoved his equipment in his bag, not even taking the time to wipe the snow off his skates. He picked up his stick and, hauling his bag behind him, made his way to the lobby. Facing the vending machine he reached into his jeans pockets and fished out some money to buy a drink.

After a big gulp, Josh turned. He saw his mother on the other side of the lobby, take-out coffee cup in hand, talking to Eric's mother. Josh gritted his teeth, hoping they were talking about something other than hockey. Why did this have to be the day his mother came? Josh felt like kicking the garbage can. He hoped she wouldn't tell his father.

After finishing his drink, Josh looked around for Kaleigh. Hopefully, she wasn't mad at him, or disappointed. Mr. Radcliffe waved and Josh gave a little nod back.

"Grab a slushie, Josh." He pointed to the canteen. "I've already paid for them." Mr. Radcliffe gave Josh the thumbs up. "You guys played great. What an exciting game!"

"Yeah," said Josh, not knowing what else to say.

"Is Kaleigh out yet?" Josh asked.

"Yeah, she's here somewhere. I know she got her slushie already." Mr. Radcliffe looked around for a few seconds. "There she is — with Eric."

Sure enough, Josh spotted Kaleigh and Eric sipping their drinks, standing close to each other in what looked like a private conversation. Kaleigh tilted her head back, laughing, making Josh wonder what was so funny. Were they talking about him? Laughing at him?

Josh felt a tug on his jacket. "Mom said to tell you to get your slushie 'cause it's time to go. You can drink it in the car."

Josh turned. "Amy, don't pull on my jacket!"

"I didn't pull on your jacket." Amy scrunched up her freckled nose. "I just told you it's time to go."

"Whatever."

"Mom told me to get you."

"Okay, Amy, I heard you."

Josh glanced back at Kaleigh but she was still talking to Eric, and now Sam had joined the conversation. Josh turned his head to see his mother throw her coffee cup in the garbage and walk toward him. She had that look on her face like, "It's time to go." Maybe he'd phone Kaleigh when he got home.

* * *

On the way home Mrs. Watson said, "Super game, Josh." She smiled at him. "It looks as if you have a good team this year. What an exciting third period."

Josh nodded.

"Josh missed the winning goal, Mom. He wasn't even there," Amy piped up from the back seat.

"Shut up, Amy," said Josh.

"I wasn't shut up, I was brought up and every time—"

Josh turned and glared at her. "I said shut up!"

"Josh and Amy, stop fighting." His mother gripped the steering wheel. "Josh, you know I hate that word."

Josh slouched in the front seat. "She started it."

"Did not."

"Did too, you little pest. I hate it when you come to my games."

"Good, then I'll never come again. I hate hockey anyway."

Josh wanted to throttle his sister. If he had been sitting in the back seat with her, he would have wrung her neck. Furious, he cranked around again. "Yeah, well at least I don't prance around a stupid stage, wearing stupid costumes, looking like an idiot."

"Joshua." Mrs. Watson's tone of voice made Josh swivel forward in his seat again.

"Why did you leave the bench, anyway?" Amy asked. "I'm telling Dad."

Josh's mom looked into the rearview mirror. "Amy, that's enough."

"Yeah, Amy, you ugly brat, that's enough."

This time Josh's mom glanced at him. "What has gotten into you?" She asked quietly.

"Nothing." He stared out the front window and didn't say another word for the rest of the drive.

When they arrived home, Josh's mom touched his arm. "Have you got homework tonight?"

Josh nodded, thinking he was going to cry. He got out of the car, ignoring Amy who was now pouting in the back seat. Opening the garage door to enter the mud room, he heard Amy say, "He should say sorry for calling me ugly."

* * *

Upstairs, Josh flopped on his bed. He had a social studies test tomorrow and didn't feel like studying. His life was a disaster! Right now, he hated everything — school, hockey, his family and Eric. Josh pounded his pillow. What was wrong with him? Why did he feel like this?

"Josh?" His mom knocked on his bedroom door. "Can I come in?"

Josh wiped his tears and rolled over to face the wall before he said, "Yeah."

His mom opened the door slowly, stepping into his room and closing the door behind her. "We need to talk."

"About what?" he said, hugging his pillow.

He heard her footsteps and felt his bed sag when she sat on the end of it. She touched his shoulder. "What's wrong?"

"Nothing."

"You can talk to me, you know."

"Nothing's wrong."

"Are you feeling okay?"

"Yeah."

"You sure?"

"Yes. I'm sure."

"Why did you leave in the third period?"

"I had to go to the washroom." He hugged the pillow harder.

"Are you having problems with this team?"

"I hate being the worst."

She rubbed his arm. "You're not the worst. And with practice, you'll get better."

"I do practise."

"Is there anything else? How's school going?"

"School's fine. School's always fine. But I don't care about school, I want to be good at hockey."

"You know, Josh, you're lucky you're so smart. Not all kids find school as easy as you."

"I don't care."

"Are you and Kaleigh still friends? Usually you chum after the game."

Josh buried his head in his hands. "I don't want to talk about Kaleigh."

"Okay." His mom stroked his hair and Josh wished he could just sit up and hug her, like when he was a little boy and he had skinned his knee. But he couldn't. He wasn't supposed to want to hug his mom anymore or cry in her arms. She kissed his cheek. "Remember, honey, I'm here for you, if you want to talk."

He nodded, still hugging his pillow.

His mom pushed a strand of hair off his face before she got up to leave. When she was at his bedroom door he said, "Mom."

She turned and smiled. "What is it, honey?"

"Is Amy in her room?"

"I just tucked her in, but she's still reading."

After his Mom left, Josh looked at his face in the mirror to see if it was red, then he went down the hall to Amy's room. Her door was wide open.

"Hey, Amy," he said standing at the door frame.

She squinted over the top of her book. "What do you want?"

"I'm sorry, okay," said Josh quickly.

Amy sat up a bit. "That's okay. I'm sorry too." She shook her head. "I promise, I won't tell Dad anything."

Josh shrugged. "Doesn't matter. He doesn't care anyway."

"I know how you feel," she said nodding her head. "He never comes to watch me dance."

"Yeah, well, I'll let you finish your reading."

"Promise you'll come to my next recital."

Josh smiled. "I promise."

When Josh went back to his room he knew he should study for his big test tomorrow. Instead he turned off his lights and crawled under his covers, fully dressed.

7

Nothing's Going Right

Josh bombed his social studies test. He couldn't seem to concentrate and every time he tried to read the questions, his vision got blurry. It was as if he needed glasses. Glasses! Josh didn't want to think about having to get glasses. If he had to start wearing glasses, he'd die. Or worse, contacts. Sam wore contacts and last year at an away tournament, Josh had watched him put them in. Sam had pulled down his eyelid and popped the lens onto his eyeball. Gross. Josh didn't think he had the stomach to do something like that to his eyes every morning.

Maybe all this blurriness was because he was tired. The last two nights, he had gotten up in the middle of the night to go to the bathroom. What was that about? He never had to get up in the night to go to the bathroom. Getting back to sleep had been hard both nights. Now he was tired, that's why his vision was blurry. When he'd gone to the optometrist six months ago, his eyes had been fine and the doctor had said he didn't need to come back for another year.

In a few of his classes, he would start to nod off then jolt himself awake. He even tried pinching himself to stay awake in English.

Josh didn't want to talk to anyone about last night's game, or the test. He opened his locker and was putting away his books when he saw Sam.

"How do you think you did?" asked Sam.

Josh shrugged, pulling out his books for his next class. "It was hard."

"If it was hard for you, then it must have been hard for everyone."

Josh closed his locker with his knee.

"I studied for two hours last night after I got home from our game," said Sam. He was not letting up.

"I got to go," said Josh. "I've got Mrs. Walsh next and she's mean if you're late."

"Tell me about it," said Sam. "I wish I had your brains. I bet you got ninety on the test."

Josh didn't know what to say. Everyone thought he was smart because his marks were always in the nineties. Wait until they saw how lousy he did on the social studies test. He thought of his parents and how they would grill him on what was wrong. If he got below eighty-five, Josh wasn't going to mention the test mark to them. Sam walked with Josh toward his class.

"We're playing a tough team next," said Sam.

Josh nodded. "I heard they were first in the standings."

"Not after we play them," Sam said with confidence. "They'll be second. The Stingers are going to take over that spot." He gave Josh a thumbs up. "We can beat them."

"Of course we can." Josh tried desperately to say his words with confidence too, but the fact was, he didn't feel confident in himself. Usually, Josh liked to hang with Sam but today he was glad to see his classroom door. He just wanted to hide behind a desk for an hour and talk to no one.

"I can't wait for our big tournament in Edmonton. We're going to play the best Alberta teams and … Coach has got passes for the water slides at West Edmonton Mall." Sam grinned.

Josh nodded. "Should be a blast."

"See you at practice," said Sam. Josh just waved.

* * *

For the next few days, Josh kept to himself. He said "hi" to everyone in the hallways, but didn't go out of his way to get together with anyone. Lately, he just didn't feel like hanging out. Not even with Kaleigh.

At hockey practice when Josh went to talk to Kaleigh, his throat got dry and his stomach felt like it was doing cartwheels. The only time he had been this nervous before was at hockey evaluations. He didn't have a clue what to say to Kaleigh, especially since all she and Eric talked about in the dressing room was the Flames game they had been to. Josh wished he had been the one at the game with her.

No one mentioned Josh leaving the bench last game; he was glad it was forgotten. Even the thought of thanking Kaleigh for sticking up for him in the dressing room was enough to make Josh break into a sweat. It was one time better left in the past.

* * *

On the day of the Stingers' next big game, Josh was heading toward Social Studies when he saw Eric and Kaleigh talking near the stairwell. Josh stopped in his tracks. He quickly pivoted, and instead took the long way to class. What if he had walked by them and they had ignored him, pretending they didn't see him? Or worse yet, said "hi," then continued talking to each other?

He hit the class before them, sat down and opened his books. The teacher stood at the front of the room, holding a big pile of papers.

"Kaleigh, Eric, sit down quickly," said the teacher. "I want to give back these tests."

Josh glanced quickly at Kaleigh, who was just coming in the door followed by Eric almost on her heels. Her seat was right beside Josh. When she sat down, Josh didn't bother to look over at her.

The teacher called out everyone's name, one by one. When it was Josh's turn, he walked up to the front, saw his mark and gulped. Sixty-four percent! He ear-marked the top corner of the test, hiding his mark, and slipped into his seat, avoiding looking at anyone.

He heard Kaleigh whisper, "What did you get, Josh?"

He shrugged but didn't look at her.

As the teacher went over the test, Josh tried to listen but his mind kept wandering to his mark and he ended up doodling all over his returned test. What did it matter? As soon as class was over, he was going to throw the test in the garbage and forget about it. Move on. Tonight the Stingers had a game.

Finally, class was over and school was out for the day. Josh picked up his books when he heard the teacher's voice. "Josh, can I talk to you for a minute?"

Josh inhaled a deep breath. He was in for it now. While all the kids filed out of the class, Josh made his way to Miss Metcalfe's desk.

"Have a seat." She pointed to a chair beside her desk.

Josh sat down, bobbing his leg.

"I'm concerned about your mark on this test, Josh."

"I didn't fail," he said defensively. His leg seemed to be moving on its own.

"I know you didn't. But you don't normally get in the sixties either." She paused. "I've noticed you seem tired, lately. Are you getting enough sleep?"

Josh traced his finger along the picture of an Asian woman on the front of his textbook.

"I don't know." Josh didn't look up.

"Maybe you should talk to your parents about how you feel."

Josh scratched the back of his neck. "Okay," he said. "Can I go now? I don't want to miss my bus."

The teacher stood and smiled. "Think about what I said."

Rushing out of the room, Josh was surprised to see Kaleigh standing by his locker.

"Hi," she said. "What did Miss Metcalfe want?"

"Nothing."

"Oh." Kaleigh held her books close to her chest and tilted her head, staring at Josh, who immediately turned his head to peer inside his locker. He grabbed his jacket off the hook. "How did you do on the test?" she asked.

"Okay," said Josh. He fumbled with his coat, dropping his books on the floor.

"I only got seventy-nine percent." Kaleigh bent over to help Josh pick up his books. "My mom is going to be mad," she continued. Josh didn't want to talk, or look at her. "She says I have to keep my marks in the eighties if I want to keep playing hockey."

Josh took his books from Kaleigh and closed his locker. "Thanks," he said. "Seventy-nine is close to eighty. I wouldn't worry about it." He turned to walk away when Kaleigh tugged on his sleeve.

"What's the matter with you?" She asked.

"Nothing." Josh pulled his arm away.

"You shouldn't have left the bench the other day in the third period."

Josh mashed his teeth together and turned to glare at her. "I couldn't help it, okay?"

"Are you feeling all right? You seem tired all the time. Maybe you should talk to your mom, you might have some sort of weird flu bug."

"I'm not sick, okay? I suck at hockey and I did lousy on the test! You happy?"

"You don't have to snap at me!" Kaleigh's eyes welled with tears. "I was just trying to help."

Josh's heart beat against his chest as he watched Kaleigh run down the hall and out the front doors of the school. He knew he had to hurry too or else he would miss the bus.

Why had he been so mean? None of this was Kaleigh's fault.

8

Family Fans

All the way home on the bus, Josh thought about Kaleigh and the hurt look in her eyes. He shouldn't have been so rude to her. She was only trying to help. He wondered if he should call her and apologize when he got home. What if she hung up on him?

Josh also thought about what Kaleigh had said. Maybe she was right — he should talk to his parents. He could speak to his mom after school. What would he say?

That he was tired? She'd tell him to go to bed earlier. If he said he was thirsty and had to go the washroom all the time she'd say stop drinking so much. If he mentioned his eyes, she'd make an appointment at the eye doctor's and Josh didn't want glasses. Last year he'd had way more sleep-overs, he went to his friends' houses all the time, played hockey on a team and on the rink outside almost every day, and he never felt tired like he did now. Last year he could play his game and come home and play for two more hours outside.

Josh stepped off the bus and immediately felt relieved when he didn't see his mom's car in the driveway. He didn't really feel like talking.

Matt was making himself a peanut butter and jam sandwich in the kitchen when Josh walked in the door.

"Where's Mom?" Josh asked.

"Errands ... with Amy." Matt shoved the sandwich in his mouth and gulped down some milk. "You ate all the chocolate chip cookies and I got blamed."

"Did she say when she was coming back?" Josh opened the fridge door and reached for the orange juice.

Matt shook his head and swallowed. "Dad phoned. He's going to take you to your game tonight."

"Really?"

"You're excited he's coming?" Matt arched his eyebrows. "Man, I wish he wouldn't come to my games. All the way home in the car he talks about the game. He's like a replay machine."

Matt broke into a Don Cherry imitation of Dad.

"Stop it, Matt," said Josh, rolling his eyes.

"I swear he tapes the entire game in his mind," said Matt. "He goes over every shot, every play. He won't even let me listen to the radio."

"You're lucky he goes to all your games." Josh sat on a stool at the kitchen island with a big bowl of cereal and a large glass of juice.

"You're the one who's lucky."

"You should be so grateful that he takes an interest," said Josh.

"Well, I'm not." Matt gulped down the rest of his milk, then wiped his mouth with his sleeve. "Hey, I don't have practice tonight," said Matt. "Maybe I'll go to your game too ... make Dad get on your case instead of mine." Matt put his plate and glass in the sink and picked up his books. He left crumbs all over the counter.

"Wow, the mighty brother at the game," said Josh sarcastically, trying not to show his excitement. He'd love to have his dad and brother at the game. Especially his brother. This might give him the boost he needed and the rest of the team would think it was cool too. He might get back in their good books. After all, Matt was a hero to them.

Josh shoved a spoonful of cereal in his mouth and glanced up at Matt. The book on the top of his pile was *Twelfth Night*.

"Hey, how did that audition thing go?"

"None of your business," said Matt.

"When will you find out if you get it?" Josh still couldn't understand why his brother wanted this role when he had scouts coming to watch him play hockey in a week's time.

"I said none of your business."

"If you get it, how are you going to do both? Have you told Dad yet?"

Matt glared at Josh. "Dad doesn't need to know right now, so don't you dare breathe a word to him. I should never have told you anything."

"When *are* you going to tell him?"

"When I get the part."

"What if he says you can't do it?"

"That's not his decision to make."

Josh knew there was going to be fireworks if Matt did make the play. He finished his juice and picked up his books, shaking his head. "I'd better get at my homework before my game."

* * *

Josh went up to his room but, instead of doing homework, he flopped down on his bed for five minutes. He heard his mom come in and when she called to him, he told her he was doing his homework. He considered what Kaleigh had said about talking to his mother. He knew his mother was downstairs unloading groceries and he could go offer to help but ... he didn't want to talk right now, not when his dad and brother were going to come to his game. He didn't want to wreck the night. Anyway, he wasn't sick.

Five minutes turned into an hour. Josh awoke with a start and looked at the clock. Geez! He hadn't touched his homework. His mom called him for dinner.

Suddenly, Josh remembered that he was going to call Kaleigh before the game. He went out to the phone in the upstairs hallway and dialed her number, tapping a pencil against the wall while waiting for the connection. What should he say to her? The phone had only rang twice when his mom called him again. He quickly hung up. "Coming," he yelled.

After dinner, the entire family piled in the SUV. Josh could hardly believe that everyone was coming to watch *him* play hockey. Even Amy!

* * *

At the arena, Josh saw Kaleigh and sped up to catch her.

"My family's here tonight," said Josh.

"That's nice," said Kaleigh.

"Kaleigh," Josh started again. "I'm sorry for the way I acted today."

"Why don't you tell someone who cares." Kaleigh rounded the corner ahead of Josh, cutting him off as she entered her dressing room without even looking back.

9

Where's the Puck?

As soon as the referee dropped the puck both teams were flying — forechecking, backchecking, skating up and down the ice at lightning speed. There was no letting up for the Stingers — one error and the Northwest Rockies would take the golden opportunity and pick up the puck. It was clear that the Rockies wanted to hold on to their first-place lead and the Stingers wanted to snatch it from their grasp.

"Short shifts, guys," yelled Coach Jim down the bench. "We need our legs. If you're tired, get off."

Josh had just come off and was breathing so hard he thought his heart would burst.

"Fast game, eh," he said to Tony, hardly getting his words out.

"We can't die out there." Tony squirted water all over his face.

Josh grabbed his water bottle but poured only enough water to wet his mouth. He was still thirsty, but didn't dare drink more. He didn't want a repeat of last game. The guys had noticed Matt in the stands and had been super friendly to Josh, especially Eric. This was Eric's big chance to show off in front of the top Midget player.

"Go, Eric!" shouted Tony.

Josh leaned over the bench so he could watch Eric stick-handle the puck down the ice. Brett lined up on the side of the net, waiting for the deflection. Josh pounded the boards in anticipation. This was it! If Eric flipped the puck over to Brett — just like last game — the Stingers could have the game opener.

Eric kept his head down and tried to weave through the two huge defense. At least they looked huge to Josh. Why didn't Eric pass to Brett?

"Pass it," Tony called. "Brett's wide open."

Eric tried to make the shot, but the defense from the Rockies had angled him into the corner and he didn't have a clear shot at the net. The puck slid out front and was picked up by the other team.

"Get back," Kaleigh bellowed.

Caught off guard, the Stingers defense skated like mad to catch the Rockies player with the puck. Josh glanced down the ice at Sam. He crouched, stick on the ice, ready for the shot. "You can do it, Sam," whispered Josh to himself.

The entire Stingers bench went silent. Everyone knew Sam was going to have make the save of the game, as the guy with the puck was one of the best Pee Wee players in Calgary. Suddenly, Eric came flying down the ice, backchecking, and hooked his stick under the guy's stick. Both players toppled to the ground and slid into Sam, pushing the net off. The whistle blew.

Everyone cheered from the bench. "Great play, Eric."

Coach Jim disliked what he saw.

"Tony, your line is out," he said.

As Josh stepped on the ice, he heard Coach Jim tell Eric to sit a shift for not passing the puck. Josh skated to right wing, telling himself he wouldn't be like Eric. He *would* pass the puck, set up the goal.

Josh bent over with his stick on the ice, ready for the face-off. He glanced up to see his family in the stands. His dad appeared relaxed, at least he didn't have his arms folded across his chest. His brother and mother were talking — not even watching the game. Josh didn't care; they would watch once the puck was dropped. He focused on the referee and Kaleigh, who was in the face-off position at centre ice. She didn't look at him. Instead, she glanced at Tony on the other wing.

Sure enough, she won the face-off, drawing it back to the left defense who fired it up the boards. Tony managed to get it on his stick and, with no other option as neither Kaleigh or Josh were yet open, he flicked it up the boards and skated around the Rockies player. Kaleigh and Josh took off down the ice. Once Tony was over the blue line, Josh drove to the hash marks. Tony passed it to Kaleigh then skated to the side of the net. Kaleigh passed it back to Tony and he deflected it into the top corner!

The crowd roared. Kaleigh and Tony jumped on each other and Josh skated over to join the huddle. He was glad to have been on the ice when the goal was scored. Matt gave him the thumbs up.

The next shift out, Josh worked as hard as he could, but his opponents just seemed to be faster and stronger. When the Stingers defense picked up the puck and circled around the back of the net, Josh positioned himself along the boards, skating forward so he could receive a pass at full tilt. His defense saw him and fired the puck up the boards. Finally, Josh had the puck on his stick!

Staying wide, Josh stick-handled along the boards, keeping his head up so he could make the pass. He saw Kaleigh striding up the ice, wide open. Josh took aim and sent the puck in her direction but … his pass just wasn't hard enough. From out of nowhere came a Rockies player. He intercepted the pass, deked the Stingers defense and headed in for a breakaway on Sam. Sam stuck out his glove, but the puck sailed by him into the top corner. Josh shook his head and skated over to Sam.

"Sorry, Sam." Josh tapped him on the pads with his stick.

"Make your passes count," said Sam. "We can't afford breakaways with this team."

Josh nodded and skated back to the bench. Coach Jim patted Josh on the helmet. "Don't throw your passes away, Josh. If you can't make the pass, shoot. Get it deep in their zone. With this team, the passes have to be on the money."

Josh grabbed his water bottle. Again the little bit of water he squeezed into his mouth was not enough to quench his thirst.

Half-way through the third period, Josh felt exhausted. He could hardly skate the length of the ice without getting winded.

On the bench, he glanced up at the clock and wished the game was over. Usually, he wanted to play and play, but today he wished the buzzer would sound. Knowing there was just three minutes left, he took a huge drink.

The score was tied 1–1. All the Stingers bench players stood up and leaned over the boards to watch the game. Josh, sandwiched between Tony and Kaleigh, couldn't keep the game in focus so he lowered his head, shaking it back and forth. Suddenly, he heard the crowd cheer. But it wasn't his bench. The other team had scored. When he glanced up, he saw Eric slam his stick on the ice.

"What happened?" Josh asked Tony.

"Our defense let them walk in." Tony moved forward, toward the gate. "We're out next. Let's make this shift count. We're only down by one."

Josh stepped on the ice, wanting desperately to feel confident like Tony. Sucking in a big breath, Josh tried to skate strong toward his wing. His line had a chance to bring the

Stingers back into the game with a tie. The team was down by one and this was probably the last shift, for Josh anyway, as Coach Jim would play the power play, the best five guys, for the last two minutes. And that wasn't Josh.

The referee dropped the puck. Kaleigh struggled with the face off and both centres scrambled for possession of the puck. It ended up on a Rockies stick. The player passed the puck up and the play was now headed for Sam. Josh skated hard, trying to backcheck, but his legs wouldn't work. "Get back, Josh! *Skate!*" his dad thundered.

He dug deep but the guy was two strides ahead, then three, then four. Fortunately, Tony caught up with him and managed to bat the puck off the guy's stick. Kaleigh swooped in, picked up the puck, and — making a tight turn — changed the direction of the game.

"Go, Kaleigh!" Josh could hear Coach Jim's voice. "Josh, get moving! Get open for her!"

Josh headed back up the ice toward the Rockies end. He watched Kaleigh thread her way through a few of the Rockies players. Then she swung over to Josh's wing. Josh followed her lead and crossed over to centre ice. She hit the blue line and he was right behind her. Now they had a two on one. Her choice was to try and deke the Rockies defense, as Eric had done earlier, which was a risk, or to make the defense come to her then throw the puck to the open man. Josh knew Tony was busy tying up the other Rockies defense. If she passed, it would be to Josh. If she managed to hit him right on, he would have a shot at an open net. This was his chance!

He smacked his stick on the ice, calling to Kaleigh. Just then, everything blurred. Josh lost sight of the puck. He put his stick on the ice anyway, still hoping to shoot it, score a goal.

When he attempted his shot, Josh heard the crowd groan.

He'd fanned completely.

Kaleigh hustled in behind him but she didn't have enough time to make a decent shot, and the Rockies' goalie pounced on the puck. The whistle blew.

On the way back to the bench, Josh snuck a glance to see his father with his arms crossed. His brother was no longer in the stands. Josh wanted to smash his stick on the ice and break it but he knew that could cost his team a penalty. Darn! He'd missed his big chance.

10

Skin and Bones

The Stingers dressing room was quiet after the game. Josh bent over to untie his skates, sweat pouring off his brow. He heard Coach Jim lock the dressing room door so the parents couldn't come in. This meant they were to have a talk.

"Stingers, all eyes on me," said Coach Jim.

Josh sat up, slouching against the concrete wall. He noticed that Kaleigh was on the other side of the room, sitting beside Eric. He looked back at Coach Jim.

"That was a tough loss," said Coach Jim. "We made a few errors and they capitalized on them." Josh lowered his head, thinking how he missed the perfect pass.

"I'm not blaming anyone," continued Coach Jim. Josh lifted his head and Coach Jim made direct eye contact with him. Josh wished he hadn't singled him out, even if he was saying it wasn't his fault.

"The Stingers are a team." Coach Jim eyed every player in the room. Some nodded; others tried to avoid eye contact. "The Rockies beat us to the puck on a few occasions and used our mistakes to win. We *can* beat the Rockies. We have to pass the puck and be sure of those passes." Once again he stopped, staring at each player.

"Hockey is a team sport, a passing game. What I'm seeing

right now in this dressing room, is a team — a great team. A team with the potential to win. But, to do that, we have to work together; every player in this room is important to our success. Now, I want to see everyone at practice on Friday at 5:00 PM. Don't be late. I want you ready to go as soon as the ice is flooded. The Rockies will be in Edmonton next weekend for the tournament. Let's be ready for them."

The sound of the door unlocking echoed in the dressing room.

After Coach Jim had left, Josh tried to get Kaleigh's attention but she wouldn't look at him. She wiped off her skates and carefully placed them in her bag. Then she stood to leave.

"Good game, Kaleigh," said Eric. "Great pass at the end." Eric glanced at Josh. "Too bad your winger didn't pick it up."

Josh thought Kaleigh might say something to Eric about it being no one's fault, but she didn't even look at Josh.

"Thanks," she said tugging her bag. "You played a terrific game too."

Josh knew his cheeks were burning. He felt like saying something about how Eric hadn't made his pass, missing an opportunity for a goal, but he didn't.

Instead, he undressed quietly. After about five minutes, some guys started fooling around, batting towels at each other. Coming out of the shower, Josh draped the towel around his waist and shook the water from his hair.

Tony smiled, rolled up his towel and flicked it at Josh. "Gotcha, line mate."

Josh laughed and tried to grab Tony's towel but missed.

"Hey, Watson," said Eric. "You look like a skeleton."

"Say what?" Josh turned to see Eric pointing at him.

"Look at your ribs, man. We can see every one of them."

Josh snatched his T-shirt off the peg and in one swoop had it over his head.

"You need a little meat on those bones," Eric said flexing a muscle. "See this?"

"That's nothing," said Sam jumping on the bench, dressed only in his boxers to flex his muscles. "Look at these babies." Sam posed like Mr. Universe and everyone burst out laughing except Josh, who took the opportunity to dress without being under scrutiny. He felt his ribs through his T-shirt. Lately, his pants had been fitting kind of big, even after they'd come out of the dryer. Maybe he should get on a weight training program. Last summer he'd gone to the gym with Matt a few times, just for fun, but he'd never lifted seriously. Matt said it wasn't necessary at his age.

Nervous as to what his father would say about the game, Josh dawdled down the hall to the arena lobby. When he walked by Coach Jim, Josh felt a hand on his shoulder.

"You okay, Josh?" asked Coach Jim.

"Yeah, sure," mumbled Josh.

Coach Jim was looking at him funny. "Go get your slushie. I paid this time," Coach Jim smiled, patting him on the shoulder.

In the lobby, Josh saw his parents standing with Sam's parents, and Matt was talking to Kaleigh.

"Tough luck," said Matt as Josh approached.

"Yeah, right," replied Josh. Out of the corner of his eye, he tried to see if Kaleigh was looking at him but she wasn't. She seemed enthralled with Matt, oblivious that Josh had even joined the conversation.

Matt slapped Josh on the back. "Don't take it so hard. Kaleigh says you play that team again in Edmonton."

"I know. It's just that—"

"I gotta go," said Kaleigh. "My parents are ready to leave and I don't even have my slushie yet."

Matt touched her shoulder. "You played a great game. Remember what I said about next year."

"I will. Thanks, Matt!" She left without even a word or a glance at Josh.

When Kaleigh had left, Matt raised his eyebrows and said, "She needs to play on a girl's team. They play a different game. I bet we see her on the Olympic Team one day. She's a great player."

"Yeah," said Josh blandly. "Too bad I missed her pass."

Matt refocused on Josh. "What did happen there? You had it. You looked like you mistimed it."

"Mistimed it? I missed it completely!" Josh shook his head in disgust.

Matt put his hand on Josh's shoulder. "Hockey's not everything, you know."

"It is to me," said Josh.

Matt punched Josh on the arm and grinned. "You're calling my bluff little brother 'cause I know that girl over there means something to you too." He leaned in, until his cheek touched the top of Josh's head and pointed to Kaleigh. "What's going on between you two? Did you do something to make her mad?"

"Don't bug me." Josh pushed away from Matt. "Where's Dad?" There was no way Matt could find out Josh had been rude to Kaleigh.

"Bringing the car around."

"Did he watch the whole game?" Josh said, flicking his stick as if he was taking a wrist shot.

"Oh, yeah, he watched," said Matt. "Lucky you though, he didn't take any notes. With me he fills a binder."

"Did he say anything when I missed that pass? Or did you even see it?"

Matt grabbed Josh by the shoulders, spinning him around to face him. "I told you, hockey isn't everything. Let it go! Anyway, it's not you Dad's mad at. It's me. The feeling's mutual."

"Where did you go?" asked Josh. Matt was full of hot air again, spouting off about Dad. "I didn't see you in the stands at the end…"

"Gimme a break. I had to get away from everyone asking about *my* hockey. They all care way more than I do. And Dad just uses me to make himself look good. I hate that!"

"I bet you didn't tell him about the audition," Josh taunted.

Matt glared at Josh. "I never should have told you." He pursed his lips for a few seconds then said, "I can't wait to tell him … see his reaction!"

Josh didn't want to think about it. Instead, he remembered what Sam had said about being skinny. Josh leaned into Matt and tried to pull his best little-brother grin. "Got any money for a chocolate bar?"

"Like I'm going to *give* you money?" From his pocket, Matt took out some change, and tossed it back in forth in his hands. "How badly does my fair lad need this pittance?" Matt asked in a British accent.

"Come on, Matt, don't be a jerk."

Matt thumped the change in the palm of Josh's hand. "You owe me. With interest. I need gas money. As of Friday, I'm officially not grounded from the car."

"The way you drive, you're going to need more than gas money," said Josh.

"Hurry up," ordered Matt. "The grump is waiting."

* * *

The ride home was horrible. Josh slouched in the middle seat of the SUV and stared out the window. His dad hardly said a word about the game except, "maybe next time." How lame was that?

Josh's mom did the gushing thing. "Good game, honey. Nice

try. What an exciting finish. You almost made that goal at the end."

Josh wished she'd be quiet; she was just trying to cheer him up. He would love for Dad to go over the game with him, tell him what he could do to be better, take some interest. For the past few weeks he hadn't said anything.

Amy prattled on about something. Josh wanted to reach over and put a muzzle on her mouth.

And Matt sat in the back with his mouth shut.

When they arrived home, Josh went straight to his room and closed the door tightly before taking off his shirt. The image in the mirror made him want to throw up. He *did* look like a skeleton! His ribs protruded and the skin covering them looked like onion-skin. He sat on the edge of his bed. He couldn't figure it out; it wasn't like he wasn't eating. Every morning, after his mother packed his lunch, Josh would sneak into the pantry and fill another bag with snacks. He'd never eaten so many granola bars and puddings before. Yet he was skinnier than ever! How could he be losing weight?

11

Excuses

All week, Josh ate — snacks, meals, sweets … but the food didn't help him put on weight. He still looked thin and felt really tired. At times, Josh would even nod off in class.

When Sam invited him over one day after school to play hockey, Josh made up some lame excuse about having to study. The fact was, Josh hardly opened his books all week. All he wanted to do was lie on the couch and watch television or nap in his room.

Sometimes when he was lying on his bed, staring at the white stucco ceiling, he would hear Kaleigh's voice telling him to talk to his mother. A few times he tried. In the kitchen, when just he and his mom were there, he'd open his mouth to talk but nothing would come out. The words seemed to get stuck in his throat like a big wad of tape.

Josh said "hello" to Kaleigh a few times at school, and she said "hi" back, but nothing else. She seemed to be spending a lot of time with Eric.

On Thursday, Josh knew he should study for the math test coming up, so after school he grabbed a snack and went up to his room. He put his books on his desk and lay on his bed to play with his Gameboy first — even though the test was worth 25 percent.

From his bedroom, Josh heard Matt come in and go to the kitchen. The banging of drawers and cupboards meant Matt was making himself a snack. Then Josh heard the garage door going up, and he knew his dad was home as well. Glancing at his clock, Josh realized that his dad was home early from work. He remembered Matt had a practice before the first big game of the Midget tournament tomorrow night. Josh couldn't wait until *his* team went to Edmonton.

Mr. Watson had only been in the kitchen for a few minutes when the fighting began. They had been at it all week. Matt had wanted the car one night, but their dad had been firm that he was grounded until Friday. Then, Matt had been late for practice one day. He'd been messing around, taping his stick.

"Would you lay off?" Matt yelled.

"Matt, you have a chance to be a great hockey player and you're throwing it all away. For what? A part in a high school play?! There are *scouts* coming to watch you. You could have a chance at a college scholarship."

Josh went to his bedroom door, opening it a crack … Matt must have told Dad about the play. Josh had heard Matt in his room, rehearsing his lines for hours on end. He must have got the part.

"Did you ever think that maybe playing hockey for the rest of my life is not what I want?" demanded Matt. "Maybe I don't want hockey to be my career!"

"You're wasting unbelievable opportunities. Maybe you don't want to go the Junior route, but don't throw away a scholarship! That's a chance for an education, Matt."

"Yeah, and I have to play *serious* hockey to get that education. I can't do anything else when I play hockey. I never played baseball, or basketball, or got to audition for *any* school play. For years I've had to play outside on *your* rink or you made me feel guilty. You enrolled me in spring hockey, summer hockey camps and nothing else. This has always been your dream, not mine!" Matt yelled.

"You're a great hockey player, Matt!" Now Mr. Watson was shouting too. "Do you know how many guys your age would kill for your talent?" He must have slammed something.

"I don't care. I don't want to perform on the ice anymore. The rush of scoring goals doesn't compare to being on stage. *I want to be an actor!*"

"You cannot make a decent living in that profession. I will not let you throw away talent or the chance for a good education! One day you will thank me for this."

Josh listened closely but all he could hear was silence. "We should leave for your practice soon." Josh could barely hear his dad. He must have taken a few deep breaths.

"Yeah, yeah," mumbled Matt.

Matt's footsteps came toward the stairs, Josh quietly closed his bedroom door and hopped back on his bed.

"Hey, Josh," Matt barged into Josh's room.

"Could you knock first? There *is* a sign on the door."

"Do you think I care?"

Josh shook his head disgustedly. "What do you want?"

"Aren't we the grumpy little skinny boy." Matt waved something that looked like tickets in his hand. "I've got a couple of extra movie passes for tomorrow night and wanted to know if you wanted them for you and your *girlfriend*."

I don't have a girlfriend." Josh picked up the Gameboy that he had thrown on the bed. "Anyway, I've got practice. Then Mom is picking me up for your game."

"Don't come to my game. I may not even be there," said Matt.

"Give them to someone else," said Josh. He wondered what

Matt meant about his game. Was he really planning on not going?

Matt shrugged and headed for the door. Josh said, "I sure wouldn't give up on my hockey if I were you."

Matt faced Josh, his lip curled up. "Not you too." He balled his hands into fists. "You sound like Dad."

"Are you going to your practice tonight?"

Matt flashed a sneaky smile. "Sure am. I need the car tomorrow. As of then, I'm officially not grounded any more."

"Dad's not that bad, you know," said Josh. "He just wants what's best for you."

"Oh, listen to the perfect child, Daddy's wannabe pet."

"Be quiet, Matt."

"It's true. You'd lick his boots to get him to watch your hockey."

Josh sat up and threw a pencil at Matt. "Get out!"

* * *

Josh studied ten minutes for his math test — not long enough, but at least he cracked the book open. He couldn't seem to concentrate and felt so lethargic. He thought of approaching his mom again, trying to talk to her but … what was the point? She couldn't do anything about it tonight, since the doctor's office wasn't open.

Josh decided to wait until the weekend was over before he broached the subject with either one of his parents. After all, it was a busy time for his parents, what with Matt's tournament, the fighting going on and Amy in yet another dance competition. The whirring sound of the sewing machine, which Mom had set up in the dining room, echoed through the house. His mother was working on Amy's costume and Josh knew well enough that now was not the time to talk to her.

Josh opened his math books once more. Stuck on a question, he decided to call Kaleigh. He let the phone ring just once before hanging up, remembering she was still mad at him.

* * *

At around 9:00, Josh was abruptly awoken by a knock on his door. He jumped up and smoothed his hair.

"Who is it?"

"It's just me, Josh," said his mother. "I wondered how your studying was going."

"Okay."

"Can I come in?"

"Sure." Josh felt funny, groggy-like.

When his mom saw him, she had a quizzical look on her face. "Were you sleeping?"

"No." Josh scratched the back of his neck.

"Are you feeling okay?" She walked over to his bed and placed a hand on his forehead. "No fever."

"I'm fine, Mom." He dodged his head to move from her hand.

"I hope you're not coming down with anything. Do you have a sore throat?"

"No. I think I stayed up too late studying last night."

"Josh, you know I like lights out at 10:00." She paused. "I want to talk to you about tomorrow night. Dad will drive you to practice and I'll pick you up. From the arena, we'll go straight to Matt's game. Fortunately, Amy doesn't dance tomorrow night. Do you want to invite a friend?"

Josh shrugged. "Maybe."

"We have room in the car … maybe Kaleigh or Sam would like to come."

"Yeah, I could ask Sam."

The mudroom door opened downstairs. "Dad and Matt must be home."

Josh heard his dad's voice. "You've got to come out aggressive, Matt. You were holding back tonight. You're big. Hit those guys! They'll be looking for the guys who can solidly hit."

"Yeah, okay. Can I drive the car to school tomorrow so I can sleep in a bit?"

Josh watched his mother pick at the lint on his bed cover, her head down, as she listened to the conversation downstairs.

"And make every shot count. Every single shot."

Josh's mom lifted her head and forced a smile. Josh had seen it before. So much for Josh talking to her about feeling tired — not with the tension between Matt and Dad.

She pushed Josh's hair off his forehead. "Get to bed, honey."

Josh nodded. At the door, his mom stopped and slowly turned back. "Josh, does Matt have a girlfriend we don't know about?"

Josh put his math books on his desk. "I don't know."

"What about these other friends of his? Do you know much about them?" she asked.

Josh shook his head. "Matt tells me nothing." Dad obviously hadn't talked to Mom about the play.

After his mom left, Josh felt a funny twinge inside. Josh knew Matt was up to something and wasn't leveling with either of his parents, but then … neither was Josh. He never did tell them about his grades slipping. He should he have told Mom about his eyes, and how he was losing weight, and how he was always so tired — so they wouldn't be surprised at report card time.

No. Josh knew that with the way things were, neither his mom nor his dad needed any more stress, at least not now.

12

Tough Test, Tough Practice

The next morning, Josh woke up late. His mother made him some toast and wrapped it in a paper towel as he rushed out of the door.

Waiting for the bus, in the dark of the morning, Josh shivered. The temperature had dropped overnight to -25°C. His breath looked like crystal. Eating his toast, his hands shook under his bulky mitts and his teeth rattled in his head. He eaten only half his toast before he dropped it on the ground.

"No!" Josh cried. He was still starving. He thought about eating some of his lunch for breakfast when he remembered that he was buying from the cafeteria today. He had a few snacks in his bag, but getting them out with his mitts on would be a nuisance.

It was too late anyway. Josh saw the headlights of the bus approaching. He wished he could go back in the house and skip the math test. He'd hardly studied and he was nervous. Twenty-five percent was a huge chunk of his mark.

On the bus, instead of pulling out a snack to eat, Josh pulled out his math text to cram. The test was first period.

* * *

When the teacher handed out the test, Josh groaned. He didn't know over half the questions! If he did poorly, he would get a lousy mark on his report card. He put his head down and got to work.

Half-way through the period, Josh's body felt weird. He rested his head in his hands and closed his eyes for a minute. He'd never felt like this before! Was it because he needed more breakfast? Josh took a few deep breaths and went back to the test.

When Josh stood, after the teacher had picked up all the test papers, he had to grab the side of the desk to keep from collapsing. His legs felt like jelly. Kaleigh walked by, and stopped in front of him.

"How did you do?" she whispered.

Even though her face was swimming in front of him, he still knew better than to complain. This was the first time she'd talked to him in so long. "Okay," he nodded.

"You don't look good," she said.

"I'm just really hungry," said Josh. "I didn't have time for much breakfast this morning."

"Want some cookies?" Kaleigh pulled a zip-lock bag that held three homemade oatmeal chocolate chip cookies out from the pocket of her jean jacket.

Josh's eyes lit up. "Sure!" Josh wolfed down one of the cookies. When Kaleigh offered him another cookie he took it without hesitating. Almost immediately he felt normal again. He looked at Kaleigh and smiled.

"Geez, Josh," said Kaleigh giggling. "Eat much?!"

Josh grinned sheepishly. "Sorry. I'm starving. Must be growing, you know." He popped the second cookie in his mouth. "Thanks," he said still chewing.

"Looking forward to practice tonight?" Kaleigh asked as they walked out of the classroom.

"Yeah," said Josh. He remembered about asking a friend to go to Matt's game tonight. He also thought about Matt giving him movie passes. What a dork. Josh would way prefer to go to a Midget game. "I'm going to my brother's game tonight. Want to come?"

Kaleigh scrunched up her face. "Sorry."

Josh felt his heart drop to his toes.

"I already told two of my girlfriends I'd go with them. Maybe we could hook up though."

Josh smiled from ear to ear. "That would be great!"

Eating a cheese string and a fruit roll-up, Josh's energy improved a little bit. He felt good with food in his stomach, but even better knowing that Kaleigh wasn't going to the game with Eric.

* * *

Practice seemed to go on forever. Josh kept having to take water breaks and Eric was not happy.

"Come on, Watson, quit dogging it." Eric skated by the bench where Josh had stopped for yet another drink.

Coach Jim blew his whistle. Josh raced to centre ice but was the last one there. He was about to do his lap when Coach Jim called, "It's okay, Josh. No lap."

Josh bit his bottom lip. He hated being babied by the coach. He got down on one knee … beside Eric.

"Coach should have made you do the lap," hissed Eric.

Josh, face flushed, tried to ignore him, but Eric continued.

"Why do you get off easy?"

Josh grit his teeth.

"He shouldn't treat you differently."

"Cut it out," Josh muttered. "I'm trying to listen."

Coach Jim pointed to the orange cones. "First to the cones picks up the puck and skates toward the net to take the shot. If you're not the first to the puck that doesn't mean you stop ... chase your opponent! The point of this drill is to keep your feet moving at all times." Coach Jim blew his whistle. "Half on one side, half on the other."

Josh was still thirsty. This thirsty business was driving him crazy. He saw Eric already at the end near the net, talking to Sam. Josh couldn't go over to the bench again. He skated to the opposite end and lined up behind Kaleigh. *Groan!* He was paired with Eric.

When it was Josh's turn, he got into the crouch that he had tried at Kaleigh's, knowing he had to get a good start. The ice in front of him blurred and he gulped. He heard the whistle and hesitated, trying to get his bearings. He heard a second whistle.

"Josh," yelled Coach Jim. "Go on the whistle."

After everyone had taken numerous turns, Josh had not won once. In fact, he hadn't come close to catching Eric. Finally, Coach Jim blew his whistle to end the drill. Josh hoped they would get a water break.

"Stay in your lines," began Coach Jim. "We're going to turn this into a team race. I want a team at either end. The first man — er, person — skates to centre, picks up a puck, and races in to make the shot. Keep shooting on the goalie until you get it in. Then skate back to your line and sit down. The first team with everyone sitting wins. Let's go!"

By the time Josh got moving, he was the last player in his line. He rested his chin on his stick watching Kaleigh take off toward centre. She picked up the puck no problem but missed her shot on the Stingers' spare goalie, Ben. On her fourth shot she managed to jab it in under Ben's pads. Josh cheered along with the other members of their team as she raced back to sit down.

When it was finally Josh's turn, his team was one ahead of the other team.

"Go, Josh!" cried Kaleigh. "You've got lots of time."

Josh skated to centre, picked up the puck and raced in toward Ben. Ben slapped Josh's first shot out of the way. Josh chased the puck and skated back to make another shot. Another miss. He could hear everyone screaming. The other team's last guy was now shooting on Sam. Josh took several shots, but Ben saved every one. Josh was getting really tired. His legs felt like mush and he had an upset stomach. Was he moving in slow motion? He couldn't tell.

Josh went into the corner to get the puck and, losing his balance, he fell. It took all his energy just to stand up. He had to make another shot. Digging at the puck, he felt a hand on his shoulder.

"It's okay, Josh," said Coach Jim. "You can stop. Practice is over."

Josh turned to see everyone already at the bench. Even Ben. How was he to face everyone this time?

Josh lagged behind while everyone else filed into the dressing room. He watched Coach Jim pick up the cones and put them away. He even watched the Zamboni flood the ice for the next team.

When he did enter the dressing room, he went directly to his spot, immediately bending over to unlace his skates. He wanted to curl up and hide.

The rest of the players joked around, throwing tape and snow at each other but not Josh.

Josh quickly undressed and was almost at the door when he felt a tap on his shoulder. He turned to see Coach Jim.

"I'd like to talk to you, Josh — when everyone's gone."

Josh swallowed.

"Have a seat." Coach Jim pointed toward the bench.

Josh sat down and stared at the floor.

He tapped his foot, listening to the door open as player after player filed out of the dressing room. He could also hear everything they said to each other.

"I wonder if he's in trouble for doing so lousy on that drill," whispered Brett to Eric.

"You know what I think," replied Eric. "He's going to get cut from the Stingers."

13

Walk Home

When every player had left, Coach Jim sat down beside Josh.

"Josh, we need to talk."

Josh stared at the toe of his boot and nodded. He could feel tears stinging his eyes. He didn't want to get cut from the Stingers.

"You're having some problems lately. Your play has declined dramatically in the last few weeks. At first I thought you were going through a slump."

Here it comes, thought Josh. How would he face anyone if he got cut? He'd have to be on another team and...

"But I don't think it's a slump." Coach Jim put a hand on his shoulder. "I'm worried about your health. I've noticed that you've lost some weight and ... you're extremely listless. Tired all the time. Have you talked to your parents about any of this?"

Choking back tears, Josh shook his head.

Coach Jim gently squeezed Josh's shoulder. "You have to talk to them, Josh. And if you don't, I will."

"I'll do it," mumbled Josh.

"You promise?" asked Coach Jim.

"I promise," said Josh softly.

"Tonight, okay? I'll phone first thing tomorrow to follow up."

Josh nodded.

"You can go now. Is someone picking you up?"

Standing, Josh finally made eye contact with Coach Jim. "My mom's coming to get me. We're going to my brother's game."

"Have fun." Coach Jim patted him on the back. "You're a good hockey player. You have tons of potential."

Right, thought Josh leaving the dressing room.

* * *

All of the Stingers were gone when Josh entered the arena lobby. And he didn't see his mom anywhere. That's odd. She said to be ready right away.

Josh was starving. Rummaging through his pockets, he managed to find enough change to buy a chocolate bar.

Then he went to the front door and looked through the glass to the parking lot. Where was his mom?

Josh popped the last of his chocolate bar into his mouth and glanced at his watch. His mom was already fifteen minutes late. Maybe Matt wasn't going to play after all! That fight at home would make them forget about Josh.

Josh had no money left for the pay phone. He saw that the door to the office was open, though, so he went in there to use the phone. He'd played enough hockey at this rink to know most of the arena staff.

Dialing, he saw Coach Jim head out the front door with his bucket of pucks, clipboard and binder. Josh listened to the phone ring and, when he heard Amy's voice saying, "None of the Watsons are available at the moment," he waited for the beeps to end.

"Hi, Mom," he said. "It's Josh; I'm at the rink, wondering

where you are." Josh felt sick to his stomach. Usually, a little food made him feel better, gave him energy, but not today.

Another ten minutes passed and Josh phoned again. Still no answer. This time he didn't leave a message. What should he do?

The walk home was far. Josh shivered, just thinking of how frigid it would be. He waited five more minutes before he decided he had no other choice but to walk home.

Thankful that he had got a new bag this year, one with wheels, he started off, pulling his bag behind him. He lowered his head to keep the wind from hitting his cheeks.

He had gone part way when he started feeling horrible pains in his stomach. He stopped and doubled over. Clutching his stomach, he vomited in a snow bank. He tried to breathe deeply to get rid of the pain.

Josh knew he couldn't stand in one spot. He had to keep moving … get home. When he started, the sun had been a big lemon ball in the sky. Now it was half gone and sinking fast. Soon, it would be completely gone. When the sun set in Calgary during the winter months, the temperature could drop drastically within minutes. Darkness came as quickly as the cold.

He started walking again, more slowly this time. He was having a hard time breathing too but it wasn't as if he was panting, like he did after a hard shift on the ice. This was different. His breathing seemed to be deep and forceful.

He ploughed on, trying to take his mind off his shivering body and terrible stomach pains. He made up plays in his mind where he was the hero — the big goal scorer. Scouts came to watch him. He scored a hat trick one game, when everyone was watching. They thought he was so amazing that he got drafted right out of Bantam for an NHL team — youngest ever. He was written up in every newspaper and even made *Sports Illustrated*. He was going to be the next Wayne Gretzky, Joe Sakic.

Josh stopped again to throw up.

He wished his mother would come. Every time he heard a car, he lifted his head, hoping it was his mom on her way to pick him up. He decided that if someone he knew went by, he'd wave them down.

No one went by.

He wanted to lie down in the snowbank and curl up in a ball. But with the cold weather, he knew he had to keep going. All he wanted to do was crawl into bed under the warm covers and go to sleep.

Finally, he rounded the corner near his home.

Looking up, he saw his house and ... the red lights of a police car!

Josh dropped his equipment and ran.

14

The Police

A lthough Josh was completely exhausted, he tried to run as hard as he could. Why were the police at his house?

He jogged up the driveway and barged through the front door.

"Mom, Dad," he yelled, gasping.

"Oh, my word. It's Josh." His mother came out from the living room. She looked at her watch then held her hand to her chest. "I was supposed to pick you up. I'm so sorry." She enveloped Josh in a huge hug, laying her cheek against the side of his head.

"You're out of breath. What's the matter?"

"Nothing," Josh mumbled.

"I'm sorry, Josh. We must have lost track of time." His mother hugged him tighter. "This is terrible, how could I have forgotten?" She ran her fingers through his hair, brushing it off his forehead. "I'm so sorry." He knew she'd been crying.

"Why are the police here?" asked Josh.

She pulled back and held his cheeks in her hands. "Your brother's in trouble." Her eyes welled up with tears.

"What did he do?"

"He was driving too fast again, on his way to some party, not paying attention, and he rear-ended a police car."

"He hit a police car? Is anyone hurt?"

"No." She put her hand to her chest. "We're lucky he's okay." She paused. "I don't know what I would have done. It's given us all quite a scare." After she wiped the tears from her cheeks, she put her arms around Josh. "Who gave you a ride?"

"No one."

"You *walked* all the way?"

Josh nodded.

She rubbed his hand. "You must be freezing! Why didn't you phone?"

"I did."

She pressed her fingers against her mouth and closed her eyes for a moment. When she opened them she said, "You must have called when Dad was on the phone. We weren't thinking straight at the time. Then the police brought Matt home." She sighed. "I've been pre-occupied since then, Josh. I can't believe how late it is already. Why don't you go upstairs and have a bath or a shower?"

"Sure, Mom."

His mom smiled sadly at him, touching his cheek again. Then she turned and walked back into the living room.

The clock chimed in the hallway and Josh looked up. Six o'clock. Matt's game was starting in half an hour.

Josh slipped out of his shoes, feeling like he wanted to throw up again. Everything was about Matt! Now his mother was so consumed with the *police* — how could he tell her he didn't feel well? Josh didn't want to let Coach Jim down. Matt always had to wreck everything.

When Josh walked by the living room he stole a quick glance at Matt, sitting between the policeman and Dad. His chin was almost on his chest.

"We have to charge you with reckless driving. You're a lucky boy; this could have been fatal," said the policeman.

Matt mumbled something that Josh couldn't hear. Josh clung to the wall. Stomach pains again. He had to get to his room.

Amy sat on the top of the stairs, her knees pulled into her chest, her arms circling her legs. Josh sat down beside her.

"What happened, Amy?" He said, out of breath.

"Matt was supposed to be here by 4:30 to go to his game," she whispered, "but he never came home. At first Dad was mad, then he and Mom got scared. Freaky like. Mom phoned all the hospitals. And Dad paced. I never seen him like that before. Then," her eyes widened as she mouthed the words, "the doorbell rang and it was the po-lice." She pronounced every syllable.

Josh thought he was going to throw up again.

"They had Matt with them," Amy continued. "He hit a police car…" Amy shook her head and put her hand to her mouth. "And totally wrecked Dad's car. He's in big trouble."

Amy looked at Josh. "Why would Matt drive so dumb? Good thing he was all by himself." Amy tilted her head. "Josh, you don't look so good. And your breath is really stinky."

"Matt shouldn't drive so fast," said Josh, closing his eyes.

"Now he can't play hockey tonight," said Amy.

"He didn't want to play anyway," muttered Josh.

Amy bunched her eyebrows together. "But Matt loves hockey."

Amy's face moved in and out of Josh's vision. He put his hand on the carpet to steady his body. He felt so sick! He knew he couldn't move. "Amy, go get me a juice box?" Josh licked his lips and pressed his fingers to his temples.

Amy shook her head, her blond braids flying like a dog's wagging tail. "No way. I'm not going down there. I don't want to get in trouble."

Josh closed his eyes.

He heard Amy babbling on about Matt. Then he felt her shaking his arm. "Josh, answer me."

He opened his eyes and swallowed. "What?"

"I said, will Matt have to go to jail?" Amy had that little girl whimper in her voice. She sounded distant, as if she was on a cell phone with bad reception.

He grabbed his stomach again, knowing he was going to be sick. He had trouble breathing again.

"I don't want him to go to jail." Amy started to cry. "I'd miss him so much."

Josh couldn't talk.

"Josh!" Amy shook his arm again.

"A drink." Josh couldn't tell if he was slurring his words or not. "I need—" The pain was too much. Josh put his head between his legs and threw up on the carpet.

"Mommy! Josh is sick!" Amy yelled.

"Josh, what's wrong with you?" Amy shook his arm.

This time Josh couldn't answer. Everything turned black.

"Mommy! Hurry!" Amy exclaimed frantically.

Those were the last words Josh heard.

15

Visitors

When Josh awoke, he was lying in a hospital bed with tubes up his arms. He stared at the liquid dripping through the tubes.

"Josh." His mother and father stood by his bed, holding his hands, crying. Even his dad had tears running down his cheeks. Josh had never seen his dad cry before.

"Mom ... Dad." His mouth felt as if he had swallowed sawdust.

"Oh honey, you're awake." His mom kissed his forehead. Then she reached over and pressed a red button by Josh's bed. "The doctor said to call immediately."

Josh glanced up at his dad, who was staring at him with a horrible, sad look on his face.

"What happened?" Josh tried to think back. All he remembered was walking home and ... Matt. And the police.

"How's Matt?" he croaked.

"He's fine," said his mom. "He's waiting outside to see you."

"Did he play his game?" Josh rolled his head to the side. It felt as if he was trying to move a ton of bricks.

Dad looked at Josh and attempted a smile but didn't say anything.

"How do you feel?" asked his mom.

"Okay, I guess." Actually, Josh felt terrible — weak, groggy and sick to his stomach. "What's … what's wrong with me?"

"Oh, honey," said his mom. "They've done some tests and," she glanced at his father before turning back to him, "you have Type 1 diabetes."

"Diabetes?"

His mom sat on the side of Josh's bed and his father stood behind her, his hand on her shoulder. "It's when your body, your pancreas, doesn't produce insulin," said his mom.

"Am I … really sick? Am I going to die?"

His mom shook her head and smiled. "No, sweetie, you're not going to die." She paused and brushed her finger along his cheek. "Without insulin you build up sugar in your blood-stream. It doesn't get converted to energy. So … you've got to put insulin in your body. Once you're feeling a little better, the doctor and nurses will help you. If you listen and follow what they say, you don't have to be sick."

"Can you play hockey with diabetes?" Josh swallowed.

Both of his parents smiled and nodded. "You can," said his mother. "You'll have to be careful but it's certainly possible." She paused. "You'll need to learn some things, though — about how to live with this." She traced a finger down his arm until her fingers were by his fingers. She looped her baby finger around his baby finger. "I should have seen the signs." She wiped at a tear.

Josh's dad squeezed her shoulder. Then Josh heard him sigh as he ran his hands through his hair.

"Your dad and I have a lot to learn as well," said his mom.

"Can I … go to Edmonton next weekend with the Stingers?"

His parents looked at each other. Then his mom said, "We

don't think so, Josh. We want you to get adjusted to this. You'll just be out of the hospital."

Josh looked away. He didn't want anyone to see the tears rolling down his cheeks.

* * *

Josh was told he had to remain in the hospital for a few days. For Saturday and Sunday, he was in the Intensive Care Unit and wasn't allowed outside visitors. It didn't matter because all he did was sleep anyway. His mother and father took turns staying by his side, day and night. Matt and Amy visited, but only for a few minutes at a time.

By the third day, Josh was feeling a lot better and they transferred him to a regular ward. His new room had a television.

He had just turned it on when the nurse walked in, carrying a basket.

Josh watched her pull out what looked like a pen. Then he found out that he had to learn how to give himself an injection with this "insulin pen." He thought of Sam putting his contacts in and how gross it was. Now, he had to give himself a needle?

The nurse handed Josh the needle and showed him exactly what to do. He squirmed. Fortunately, his mother immediately came to the rescue. The nurse said it was perfectly okay for his mom to give him the injection until Josh got used to doing it himself. Mom stuck the needle in his thigh. He had to have this injection three times a day!

After the needle demonstration, the nurse pulled out a little black kit. When she opened it, Josh saw something that looked like a stop watch. The nurse explained that it was a blood monitoring kit. Four times a day, Josh had to prick his finger to check his blood sugar level. His own first jab didn't penetrate the skin.

The nurse smiled, her eyes crinkling in the corners, and encouraged him to just try again. She was patient with Josh, reminding him of Coach Jim. On his second try, Josh was successful.

Each time he pricked his finger, Josh had to record his level in a little book. He learned that if his blood sugar was below four he needed to eat some candy, drink a pop or juice or pop a glucose tablet into his mouth.

Five minutes after the nurse left, a dietitian visited. She explained to Josh that he would have to follow a meal plan. He had to watch what he ate, and eat at specific times. No skipping meals.

Josh listened carefully because she was so nice, but when she left he flopped back against his pillow and closed his eyes. Why was this happening to him?

"Want to play chess, Josh?" his dad asked.

Josh opened his eyes and sat up. He hadn't even heard his dad enter the room. He shrugged. "Sure."

"I'm going to get a coffee," said his mom.

"I'll set up," said his dad, putting the chess board on Josh's bed.

Josh watched in silence as his dad organized the pieces.

"You go first," said his dad, finally looking up.

Josh moved his knight. His dad countered with a pawn. The play went back and forth for at least five moves before anyone said anything.

And it was Dad who spoke first. "Listen, Josh." His dad had just moved his queen. He wrung his hands. "I'm sorry I didn't see what was happening to you."

"That's okay," said Josh, eyeing his next move. "You, uh, left your queen open," he mumbled. He had a huge lump in his throat.

"No, it's not okay," said Dad. "I should have been more involved."

"You had Matt to think about," said Josh, shrugging, still looking at the chess board.

"It was wrong of me to focus all my attention on Matt."

Josh could feel his eyes welling up. "Why did you then?" he whispered.

"Look at me, Josh."

Josh shook his head.

His dad reached over and gently took Josh by the shoulders, pulling him close. Josh buried his head in his dad's chest.

"I'm so sorry, Josh," said his dad, running his hands up and down Josh's back. "I promise, I'll make it up to you."

* * *

Around 4:00 PM, Josh found himself wondering what all his friends were doing after school. His dad had already told him that the Stingers had won their game on Sunday. They were probably getting ready for Edmonton.

Josh missed his friends. Now that he was feeling better, he wished some of them would come see him to relieve the boredom.

Josh fell back against his pillow. None of this was fair. Why did this happen to him? Josh thumped his hand against the bed. Why didn't it happen to someone else?

Josh was flicking through the television channels when he heard a voice at his door.

"Hey, Josh."

He sat up to see Eric standing with his hands behind his back!

Eric awkwardly walked into the room and stood beside Josh's bed. "I'm here on behalf of the team." From behind his back he pulled out a white envelope and a present wrapped in comic papers. "It's the only paper I could find," he said. "A girl suggested I use comics for fun."

"Kaleigh?" Josh asked, his heart beating against his chest.

"Lauren. She's my new girlfriend," said Eric proudly.

Grinning at this information, Josh sat up and took the gift. "You can sit down, you know."

"Sure." Eric sat on the side of Josh's bed.

Every player on the team signed the card. Josh turned it upside down and sideways, smiling as he read their notes. Everyone hoped he would soon be back to play hockey for the Stingers.

Opening the present, Josh was thrilled to find over a dozen packs of hockey cards. "Thanks!" He grinned.

"Let's open them," said Eric. "See who you got."

One by one, they opened every pack, talking about every player. They read the stats on the back and put them in groups: singles, duplicates and, of course, stars.

"Next time I come visit," said Eric, "I'll bring mine and we can trade."

"I'm getting out tomorrow or Wednesday," said Josh.

"Maybe you can come to my house and we can trade. That is, if you're feeling okay."

"The doctors have all said I'll be fine."

"What *exactly* is wrong with you?"

"I have diabetes. Actually, it is called Type 1 diabetes."

"What's that mean?"

"There's this thing called a pancreas in our bodies. It's an organ, like the kidneys, liver. Remember we learned some of this in health?"

"I probably wasn't listening," said Eric.

"Anyway, the pancreas produces insulin, which keeps the blood sugar in our bodies okay. Mine doesn't produce insulin, so from now on, I have to give myself a needle three times a day."

"Every day?! Three times! Really?" Eric's eyes were wide. "Oh, man. I don't think I could do that."

Josh rolled his eyes. "I don't have a choice. Nurses have been in here all day, drilling me on everything. But they're nice."

"Is it hard?"

"What?"

"To give yourself a needle?"

Josh shrugged, thinking of how he had to get his mom to do it. "Sure it's hard," he said with big attitude. "But nothing I can't do."

"You're amazing," said Eric. "Hey, can you still play hockey?"

Josh nodded hesitantly. "Yeah. Just not this weekend."

Eric glanced at his watch and put on his coat. "I got to go. My mom said she'd pick me up in an hour."

Josh tried to smile. "Thanks again for stopping by."

"Whatever," Eric shrugged, zipping up his coat. He stood by Josh's bed for a few seconds, jiggling his leg. "Josh, I ... I just wanted to say sorry for being such a jerk to you. I didn't know you were sick."

"It's okay. I didn't know I was sick either," said Josh.

"Well, I hope you get better soon. We'll miss you in Edmonton this weekend. You're still part of the team, you know. You're still a Stinger."

"Beat those Rockies," said Josh, trying to hide his disappointment at not being able to go.

"We will." Eric gave Josh the thumbs up.

* * *

After Eric left, Josh read all his hockey cards again, then dozed off. When he woke up he saw Kaleigh coming in his room with a big bunch of helium-filled balloons, a hockey stick and a brightly wrapped present.

"Hi, Josh," she said, sitting on the end of his bed. "I hope I didn't wake you. I saw your parents in the lounge and they said it would be all right if I came in. They figured you'd be awake soon." She paused. "How are you?" She asked quietly.

"I'm okay." He forced his smile.

"I'm sorry to hear that you got so sick."

"Who told you anyway?"

"Coach Jim, at practice on Saturday. He phoned your house that morning and talked to your brother. I think your parents were at the hospital at the time. Then Coach went to the hospital before practice and spoke to your mom and dad." She paused for a moment, then said softly, "We were all pretty scared for you."

"I didn't know what was wrong with me," he said. "How was practice?" Josh changed the subject.

Kaleigh shrugged. "Good. I missed you though."

"Really?"

"Yes, really." Kaleigh gave him a gentle jab on the arm. "I like you, Josh. You're fun."

"Really?"

Kaleigh playfully pursed her lips, shaking her head. "Of course."

"Here," she said. "I brought you a present."

Josh cranked his bed up to take the present from Kaleigh. "Cool bed, eh?"

"You got a television too." She pulled the little television over. "Wow — it moves!" She looked around. "I've never been in a hospital."

"Me, either, till now," said Josh. He curled his lip. "The food sucks. And you *need* a television. It's really boring. I sleep a lot though. And lots of people come in to talk to me. Plus my family's here all the time." He started to unwrap the gift. "My parents said I can't go to Edmonton, but I can play when you guys get back."

"Coach Jim told us the same thing. He said if you follow the doctors' orders, you'll be fine. Good as new." She bobbed on the bed. "I hope you like what I got you."

Ripping open the wrap, Josh beamed when he saw the hockey trivia book."

"Thanks."

"I thought you might need something to read." She grinned mischievously. "Ask me any question from the book; I bet I know the answer."

"I bet you don't." He opened the book, thinking maybe a few things in his life hadn't changed. Kaleigh was still Kaleigh.

16

Moving Forward

Josh arrived home on Wednesday to a front entrance filled with balloons and a big banner that said, "Welcome Home, Josh." He knew immediately, from the swirls in the letters, that Amy had been responsible for the sign. Josh swallowed and wiped the tears from his eyes. All this for him. Everyone was happy to have him home.

"Hey, Josh," said Matt. "Come on out back for a minute."

"It's freezing outside."

"Yeah, but Dad and I have something to show you." Matt smiled. "Leave your coat on; it will only take a minute."

They walked around to the back, the cold air hitting Josh in the face.

When they got to the back, Josh saw the boards and ... ice!

"Our rink is ready," said his dad, stepping on the ice. "We still have a few bumps in the corners but other than that it's pretty good. Right, Matt?"

"We watered this sucker day and night," said Matt. "Man, it's a lot of work to get a rink going."

"I can't wait to skate," said Josh enthusiastically. "It feels like forever since I've played hockey."

* * *

As soon as he arrived home from school on Thursday, Josh dug out his skates. It had been weird to go back to school. All the teachers and kids were super nice to him — even kids he hardly knew.

Josh was a bit nervous tying up his skates. What if he couldn't play hockey any more? All the Stingers were excited about the tournament in Edmonton. Some were missing school the entire day on Friday, so they could check in to the hotel early. The first game was at 5:00.

Josh snapped on his helmet, grabbed his gloves and stick, and headed onto the ice. The first cut of his blade gave him goosebumps, even though his legs felt wobbly. He skated a few slow laps before he picked up his pace. The cold air on his face tingled his skin. He got low and lengthened his stride, taking the corners on his edges. He loved the sounds his skates made.

He picked up a puck and stick-handled up and down the ice. "And he's coming in, over the blue line, toward the net … he dekes the defense. Now it's a one-on-one. He shoots, he scores!" Josh grinned, it felt so good to be on his skates again.

"Why don't we set up some pylons?" asked Matt.

Josh hadn't even heard Matt come outside … with his skates on.

"I thought you hated hockey," said Josh, turning to stare at his big brother.

Matt shook his head. "I don't hate hockey. I like hockey. I'm just not sure I want to make it my career." Matt looked around. "I love this part. Being outside … hacking around. Come on, let's set up the cones. I'll teach you a great move."

Josh couldn't believe his ears!

They played for half an hour. Matt taught Josh how to deke with his shoulders to fake out the defense. At first, Josh found the move hard, but Matt was patient. He kept encouraging him until finally Josh managed to get by Matt.

"Great shot!" Matt whistled. "Right in the five hole."

Josh grinned. It was a good shot! He skated over to the chair for a break. "That was fun!" said Josh, glancing at Matt who was standing in front of him, resting his chin on his stick.

"Listen, Josh." Matt started fiddling with his stick, slapping at little ice chips. "Maybe if ... I hadn't been so crazy with the car, you wouldn't have had to walk home and get so sick that Mom and Dad had to call the *ambulance*."

"Why were you going to a party instead of your game?" Josh stared at his brother.

Finally, Matt made eye contact with Josh. "I didn't want any more pressure. I want more in my life than just hockey."

"You hit a police car ... totalled Dad's SUV..." Josh bit his lip, trying not to break out into a grin. "That's really dumb, Matt."

"I'm paying for it now." Matt shook his head. "I can't drive for three months. *And* I have to take a safe driving course."

"You need to take a safe driving course. Slow down." Josh paused for a few seconds before he said seriously, "You could have killed yourself."

Matt sadly smiled. "I know that. When the cops read me the stats, I knew I was lucky."

"Are you really going to quit hockey and join a house league?" Josh waited for the answer to this question.

Matt rocked on his skates. "I want to do the play," he said. "I want to give it a shot. My school does the best productions in the city and rehearsals take up time. It's not fair to my team if I'm not there all the time. I may go back next year. Who knows?"

"Dad ... actually seems okay with all of this," said Josh.

"Your sickness coming at the same time as me bashing into the back of a cop car made him think. I mean, come on, the police and an ambulance all in one night!" Matt rolled his eyes. "This place was hopping, let me tell you."

"Sorry I missed the action," said Josh, tapping the ice with his stick.

"Dad and I had a long talk in the hospital when you were so sick," said Matt. He paused, stopped rocking and looked at Josh. "We are all worried about you."

Josh shrugged and lowered his head.

"Dad told me I should do what makes me happy, not what he wants," said Matt. "I know it was hard for him to say that. He had his dreams for me — a son in the NHL." He raised his eyebrows at Josh. "You know, he also said he was wrong not to make a rink for you. That's when I said I'd help."

"Am I supposed to say thanks now?" Josh raised his eyebrow.

"Yeah," said Matt sarcastically. "I didn't know it was so much work."

Josh stood and skated a few strides before he said, "If I had told Mom and Dad right away I wasn't feeling so hot, I probably wouldn't have ended up in the hospital." Now he flicked at the ice chips.

"You knew you were sick?" Matt looked shocked. "That makes us both kind of lame."

"Do you think," Josh squinted into the sun to look at Matt, "*I* can make it in hockey?" Josh couldn't help be worried about his hockey.

"You know the saying, "practice makes perfect." The way you played just now, deking me out like that, I'd say sure. Plus, it takes more than talent to be good." He put his hand against his chest. "You got to have it here. I didn't have it any more. Sometimes I wonder if I ever truly had the passion."

"When did you get so philosophical?"

"You want me to play with you or not?" Matt paused.

"You've got the passion, little brother. That will take you a long way."

"I need the skill though," said Josh longingly.

Matt wagged his finger at Josh. "I bet by the end of the year, you're one of the best players on your team." Matt shook off his glove, stuck his hand out and arched his eyebrow. "Want to bet? Twenty bucks!"

Josh too shook off his glove, tucking it under his arm. Then he slowly stuck out his hand but, when Matt went to shake it, he pulled it away and laughed. "I'm not betting you because I just might lose. You're right, Matt, I'm not going to let a little interference get in my way. Come on, let's play some more one-on-one."

Other books you'll enjoy in the Sports Stories series

Ice Hockey

❏ *Two Minutes for Roughing* by Joseph Romain #2
As a new player on a tough Toronto hockey team, Les must fight to fit in.

❏ *Hockey Night in Transcona* by John Danakas #7
Cody Powell gets promoted to the Transcona Sharks' first line, bumping out the coach's son, who's not happy with the change.

❏ *Face Off* by C. A. Forsyth #13
A talented hockey player finds himself competing with his best friend for a spot on a select team.

❏ *Hat Trick* by Jacqueline Guest #20
The only girl on an all-boy hockey team works to earn the captain's respect and her mother's approval.

❏ *Hockey Heroes* by John Danakas #22
A left-winger on the thirteen-year-old Transcona Sharks adjusts to a new best friend and his mom's boyfriend.

❏ *Hockey Heat Wave* by C. A. Forsyth #27
In this sequel to *Face Off*, Zack and Mitch run into trouble when it looks as if only one of them will make the select team at hockey camp.

❏ *Shoot to Score* by Sandra Richmond #31
Playing defense on the B list alongside the coach's mean-spirited son is a tough obstacle for Steven to overcome, but he perseveres and changes his luck.

❏ *Rookie Season* by Jacqueline Guest #42
What happens when a boy wants to join an all-girl hockey team?

❏ *Brothers on Ice* by John Danakas #44
Brothers Dylan and Deke both want to play goal for the same team.

❏ *Rink Rivals* by Jacqueline Guest #49
A move to Calgary finds the Evans twins pitted against each other on the ice, and struggling to help each other out of trouble.

❏ *Power Play* by Michele Martin Bossley #50
An early-season injury causes Zach Thomas to play timidly, and a school bully just makes matters worse. Will a famous hockey player be able to help Zach sort things out?

❏ *Danger Zone* by Michele Martin Bossley #56
When Jason accidentally checks a player from behind, the boy is seriously hurt. Jason is devastated when the boy's parents want him suspended from the league.

❏ *Ice Attack* by Beatrice Vandervelde #58
Alex and Bill used to be an unbeatable combination on the Lakers hockey team. Now that they are enemies, Alex is thinking about quitting.

❏ *Red-Line Blues* by Camilla Reghelini Rivers #59
Lee's hockey coach is only interested in the hotshots on his team. Ordinary players like him spend their time warming the bench.

❏ *Goon Squad* by Michele Martin Bossley #63
Jason knows he shouldn't play dirty, but the coach of his hockey team is telling him otherwise. This book is the exciting follow-up to *Power Play* and *Danger Zone*.

❏ *Ice Dreams* by Beverly Scudamore #65
Twelve-year-old Maya is a talented figure skater, just as her mother was before she died four years ago. Despite pressure from her family to keep skating, Maya tries to pursue her passion for goaltending.

❏ *Interference* by Lorna Schultz Nicholson #68
Josh has finally made it to an elite hockey team, but his undiagnosed type one diabetes is working against him — and getting more serious by the day.